Love & Lust

Arian Mabe

This is a collection of short stories focusing on straight erotic pairings with furry characters.

This collection covers: straight sex, oral sex, vaginal sex, anal sex, BDSM, domination/submission, bondage, multiple partners, semi-public & public sex, love, romance and relationships.

Table of Contents

Mornings with Poppy

Poppy was like no one else in the world. Dylan knew that sounded like he was being overly romantic and whatnot, but he really meant it. The leopard was so long and lean, as if her limbs went on forever. Though she was a stranger leopard than many that were found in the world with her spots inverted. Where most had a golden base to their fur, she had a black base – with white rosettes layered over the top. Her eyes gleamed blue, though there was always an easy smile on her lips, gentle and ready.

She might have been a feline with sharp teeth, a huntress, but there was no malice in her, no harm at all. Dylan smiled, the bottlenose dolphin anthro opening his beak to chatter lightly, drawing her attention to where she was looking out over the sea through a telescope. It was one of those set up on coastal paths where you had to pay to take a look, but they seemed to be the only ones out there on that particularly blustery day.

The sun rose over the horizon, splashing the sea in shades of orange and pink. That sort of morning was said to promise a storm coming and he felt it in the wind too, his blowhole on the back of his head puckering and pulling lightly as he breathed. Taking her on holiday, even if it was only for a weekend before they had to return to the business of life and work together, was always a good thing. Dylan only wished he got to do it more often, though hoped that would change. All so he could spend even more time with his sweet, sassy feline.

Poppy caught him staring at her and straightened up again, her scarf fluttering lightly around her neck as it flicked back and forth. She smiled as the wind toyed with it.

"Something caught your eye?"

Her tone was light and flirtatious and even she heard it. She swung her hips subtly as she cuddled up to her partner again, sliding her arms around the dolphin. With a layer of blubber on his body, Dylan didn't need to wrap up as warm as she had. Fortunately for them, it was spring and the warmer months were indeed coming. She wouldn't need her scarf for all that much longer, for which Poppy was very grateful.

Dylan sucked in a sharp breath and she grinned, whiskers quivering. He always reacted when she leaned up against him like that, even though she was fully clothed at the time, her feline tail swishing playfully back and forth. Even with the wind ruffling her fur, the warmth of merely being close to him felt like all she needed.

The dolphin gulped a little, throat working, though that was merely an anthro reflex. Dolphins rarely needed to work their throats quite like that, catching fish naturally in their teeth and he did it more as a practised little habit than anything else. Little things like that, after all, conveyed information in body language too.

He kissed her lightly, needing to draw back his head a little, even though he only had a shorter dolphin-like beak. His tail swung lightly behind him, balancing them both, and Poppy melted against his chest.

"Mmm..."

The leopard hummed softly into the kiss, the hint of a purr in the back of her throat. Her head swam pleasantly and Poppy, for a moment, forgot where she was. The leopard forgot she was out in public, kind of, and nuzzled down from his beak to his neck. Her sharp teeth nipped and pulled at his sensitive skin. It never ceased to amaze her just how smooth the dolphin's skin was. It was so different to her own flesh and she could barely get down to her own skin when she pushed back her fur, only able to expose a very small amount at any time.

She wasn't thinking straight, the early morning still leaving her with a hint of sleep on her whiskers. Poppy's paw trailed down his chest, fingers splayed out, working their way down to his lower abdomen.

"Ah – Poppy?"

Dylan withdrew that time, lips slightly parted in surprise, although there was nothing he wanted to change about the situation. His heart pounded and he grunted quietly, for the leopard had that certain look in her eye.

She was a predator and a huntress always knew what she wanted. Licking her lips, Poppy purred throatily, her tail swinging softly back and forth.

"What is it?" She murmured, her voice low and husky. "I thought you were trying to start something."

Dylan had to clamp down his beak around a nervous chatter.

"Or, we can just do what you planned and go out to breakfast now," Poppy said, continuing as if that really was an option. "You think that'd be a better idea? I don't know, you were already getting a little – eeeeep!"

She squealed happily as he scooped her up in his arms, cradling her to his chest. Yet Dylan pulled her in more tightly than usual and grinned open-mouthed as Poppy nestled in against him, perfectly safe and happy there.

"Oh, I think the choice is all yours, sweetie," he laughed, his words barely coming through his mirth. "You know what you're doing, you little minx…"

"What – no! I'm a leopard, not a minx!"

Yet he carried her back from the lookout, the sea choppier with the wind in the background, but neither of them minded that. The day was ripe for them to glean all they wanted from it. For the moment, however, all the couple wanted was one another.

And that was okay too, even if they'd get coffee and pancakes at that little beach café another morning. There was time enough for them to spend it exactly as they willed and Poppy laughed as he carried her back to the hotel.

It had been a little steeper in cost than what they usually went for, but it was all worth it for a touch of luxury together. The hotel was on the seafront, with the harbour curving around to the other side, though it was not a harbour that was still used for fishing, so they were fortunate that there were no unpleasant strong smells on the air. Even though both of them loved fish, they didn't want to be inhaling the aroma of it all the time, after all!

It was a picturesque spot and it didn't seem many were around the area, that early in the season, which suited them fine. They skipped past the hotel reception desk on the ground floor and headed straight up to their room.

On the elevator, however, there was time for her to pin him back against the wall and kiss him hungrily. Their lips had to do a little more work to meld together easily but they made it right for them, tongues lashing out frantically together as that lure of heat built between them.

Poppy moaned into his mouth, her heartbeat pounding, though it felt more like a flutter in her chest when Dylan was with her. The dolphin did wonderful things to her and, to be honest, she had really thought he was trying to start something with her. In the end, it turned out they were simply in tune with one another, knowing intrinsically that they didn't really want to head over to breakfast after their little early morning walk.

To make the most of their weekend away, they had to spend moments together. They stumbled in one another's arms down the hallway, though their room was, thankfully, not that far. Dylan grunted as he tried to open the door with the keycard, despite still keeping her in his arms, not willing yet to let go of him.

He groaned, finally tumbling back into the room with Poppy. The feline quivered in his arms and it was all he could do to drop her lightly on the bed rather than crash down immediately on top of her himself.

"Ah…"

He breathed, coming over her more gently, arms quivering with the effort it took to support his body over the leopard. She twisted under him, sprawling out, her clothes already a mess.

"You just wanted to come back up here to spend more time in bed, didn't you?" He teased, cupping her cheek and tracing the outline of her right side of her muzzle gently. "Such a cat…"

She kissed his fingers, her tail swishing back and forth across the bed, ruffling over the bedsheets. They were some of the nicest things she'd slept on, though it was made all the better for being with Dylan. There really wasn't anyone else she'd have wanted to spend a weekend holiday with.

"Mmm, you could say," she murmured. "But I wouldn't have wanted to stay in bed for longer if not for you. Besides, that little walk in the fresh air helped me get my second wind."

He laughed and she stretched up over her head, pushing her chest out as he slowly undressed her. There was nothing quite that could ever match up to the feeling of him undressing her, everything about the dolphin so tender and so sweet. It was as if he was always putting her first, little things rising and drawing her attention.

Like how he nuzzled around her belly button when he was undressing her.

The tickle of the tip of his beak tracing a path down over her crotch.

How he caressed her thighs even as he slid her panties down her long legs.

There was a soft scent to him too, not exactly fishy but with a lick of salt to it. It spoke of the ocean and, even though she wasn't a huge fan of swimming, Poppy loved relaxing at the seaside. Even though it was early in the season for them to be heading to the coast, she still felt more at ease for simply being near the water.

And it was even better with her lover there, Dylan more hastily stripping himself down to match her. The only article of clothing left on the leopard for the moment was her bra and he would take that off in due course too.

The dolphin was a creature of beauty too as he stripped down, however. Even though his body was long and lithe, the lack of any fur on his body meant that every inch of muscle on him was nicely defined, leaving nothing at all to her imagination. Not that Poppy would have minded some things being left to her imagination too, though the leopard watched anyway, resting her head back on her arms, fingers folded under the back of her skull.

His shirt went first, revealing a bare, moderately broad chest, as smooth as silk. Yet his skin clung to every single muscle there, showing off his tight pecs and the lines of his abdominal muscles further down. There was even a line to highlight the edge of his obliques.

The heat within her burned.

Next came his trousers and underwear, though the dolphin hastened through getting his jeans off.

They were tight and restrictive for him more often than not and Dylan enjoyed summer more when he could wear shorts. His legs were smooth skinned too, yet his thighs rounded out thickly with muscle, his calves with a subtle, appealing bulge. Although he had feet, a feature of being an anthro who had evolved from their ancestors over many, many years, he still had a tail. That tail helped him to power through the water when he was in it and, otherwise, assisted him with balance walking around too.

Once, she'd asked Dylan if he would have preferred to just be an aquatic mammal, but he'd said no to that. At the time, the Bottlenose dolphin had cited not being able to meet her if he'd spent his whole life in the water, but she thought he liked life on land much more than that. There were many types of anthro in the world with all kinds of bodies – but Poppy was merely grateful for him being exactly the way he was.

"You look amazing, darling…" She purred, swishing her tail back and forth. "I wish we'd done this last night. I was just so tired after the drive."

He laughed, moving over her once again, nuzzling into her neck.

"Oh, and like I didn't crash out on the bed too?"

They laughed together and Dylan rolled her over, so the feline was on top of him. Her legs went to either side of his hips and she sat up on top of the Bottlenose dolphin, kneeling there as the slit at his crotch slowly parted with his shaft.

It let out his cock readily and easily, though the dolphin had been more than a little horny when they'd been pressed up against one another, looking out over the ocean. It didn't matter what they were wearing as he'd always want the leopard in every way and any way.

But the way she grasped his cock and curled her fingers around it was simply exhilarating. A chatter burst from his lips and clicks from his echolocation system, but Dylan wasn't trying to use it at that time. His head simply swam luxuriously as she rubbed his cock up and down, slowly coaxing him to full hardness with her paws.

The leopardess could have done more in that moment and yet he didn't need anything else, clicking and rapping the edges of his beak together as need overcame him. It was easy to forget everything when he was with her. His cock rose into her touch as if they were made to come together, the undulating length curving softly against her palm as it grew. The head of his cock tapered softly to a rounded tip, a slit in there, although it did not drool any pre-cum yet.

That would come in time as they explored one another's bodies, slowly and playfully. Who knew if they were going to get out to breakfast that day or even brunch – hey, room service was a thing! But it'd mean they'd have to get their clothes on in time to answer the door, which could be problematic.

Either way, they'd find a way to make sure their needs were met as required. The moment was theirs and he rocked helplessly up into the clutch of her fingers as they teased around his shaft. She couldn't close her paw all the way around his shaft, but it was more than enough in the moment for them both, a smile on her lips as she toyed with him. Poppy had more than one feline trait about her too.

She could play with him like a cat as she purred and nuzzled down to his cock. On all fours, she kissed the head of his cock as she bowed her head down reverently. The time they spent together was sacred as she moaned and parted her lips.

Sliding only the tip of his shaft between them, she sucked him inside her mouth slowly. Her tongue cradled his length, allowing it to tease deeper and deeper. Yet the feline didn't quite take him into the back of her mouth yet, no – she had far sweeter things in mind than even that.

Poppy purred around his cock, letting the deep, throaty vibrations roll into his cock as she sank lower and lower. Her lips parted around him, taking him seductively into her mouth, though it was fortunate that the leopard's tongue, while rough, was not as barbed as feline tongues had once been. As it was, it allowed him another delicious pull of sensation and she gulped around him, letting the back of her throat toy with the very tip of his cock.

But only that, not even as the dolphin squirmed and puffed out air through his blowhole. His toes curled and flexed, bowing his tail back and down against the bed, although he didn't use his leverage to work himself free from her. He didn't want to take control, clearly, for control like that was passed back and forth between them, depending on the scene they wanted to play out.

"Oof, Poppy… That… That feels…"

He couldn't get out the words, not as his tail flicked up between his legs, brushing against her. Yet Dylan didn't need to, parting his beak in an awed smile. Just how did she do all that she did? Even in his mind, it sounded clunky, but he enjoyed more than that, wanting her to know, all so he could appreciate her in every single way.

He didn't want to be on the bottom forever, however, his hips rolling up lightly, pushing his cock just a little deeper into her mouth. Her tongue curled and flicked around him, dragging back up against the sensitive tip, even if most of his shaft was just as tender. It was only the base, pressed right up to the slit from which it emerged, that was perhaps not quite as sensitive as the rest of his length.

It was sheer euphoria to have her mouth around his cock, bobbing her head slowly and sensually up and down, taking everything at her own pace. He only affected the pace ever so slightly with the thrust and grind of his hips, but there was still more to come, so he did not push things too much.

Dylan didn't need to, not as she ran her paws over his thighs. They often referred to her hands as paws and his as hands, but the terms, for anthros, were fairly interchangeable. Nobody really minded what was said, though they had said it was weird for dolphins to be considered as having "paws." And they couldn't call them "fins" on Dylan!

It was weird where his head went when he was trying to hold back, warmth bubbling at his core. It curled and twisted through him like the currents in the ocean and yet the dolphin could not take himself away from the moment for anything other than a few seconds at best.

"Ah… Poppy, please," he huffed, puffing out a sharp blow of air. "I need you… Only you."

She knew what he meant as she rose from his cock, a string of saliva connecting her lips, briefly, to the tip of his shaft. The feline purred and licked her lips salaciously, having drawn a drop of need from the dolphin too in the form of his pre-cum.

"Mmm… You taste wonderful, sweetie," she purred, licking her lips again but more showily that time, letting him see the pink lash and pull of her tongue in all its glory. "But I need more than just your cock in my mouth too. Maybe you can fill my throat later."

She phrased it as if it was a fact rather than a question, that she was going to get him to blow straight down her throat exactly when she wanted him. Dylan gulped visibly, his tail waving a few inches back and forth from where it was stretched out between his legs.

"Anything you want, honey," he managed to force out, his throat tight with the force of his need. "Come here, ride me. I need to feel you on my cock."

She did just as he asked and he lifted his head and torso from the bed. Although the position forced him to contract his abs, he wanted to see her in all her splendour – and that meant unhooking her bra too. Dylan just about freed her breasts as they fell forward, though it was up to Poppy to slide the straps off her shoulders and free herself from the rest of it. Her breasts bounced lightly, heavy and full, though it was the pink nipples they were tipped with that caught his attention the moment they were exposed.

His hands swept back up her body to her breasts as he fell back, unable to keep his body curled up in such a position for too long. Yet her pussy had not yet descended on his cock, hovering so close to the head of his shaft that he could feel the heat rising from her cunny too.

She slipped on to him slowly and patiently as her pussy stretched around him. He gasped, blowhole puckering and flaring, although the dolphin was right where he wanted to be. He took her deeply, though it was all up to the leopard as to how much of his cock she took and how deep she stayed.

For Poppy hissed through her teeth and rocked on his cock, rising and falling as her pussy got used to his girth. She clenched around him when she should have relaxed, though that was not such a bad thing. It only meant it was a little more difficult for her to take the length of his cock, easing more and more up inside her.

Eventually, however, he bottomed out inside her, a sliver of his shaft remaining outside her pussy.

His cock gleamed with her arousal as she rose and fell on his cock, squeezing around him more easily as her body accommodated him.

She moaned, her lower jaw falling a little slack, though her tongue remained tucked inside her mouth. Poppy tried to roll her hips a little so she could grind her clit against his cock, teasing a little, though it was a difficult position for anyone to get into. She more often than not needed her fingers to stimulate her clit, especially when his crotch was as smooth as it was.

Dylan took charge of that for her, rubbing her clit lightly, and she yowled into his touch, a shuddering buck of her hips shoving her pussy forcibly against him. With the morning rays of sunshine growing stronger through the window, he rolled her over on to her back, letting her legs come up around his waist.

In that position, they could move together a little more easily, the flexible feline wrapping her legs around his waist tightly to pull him into her. She would have got every last stroke she wanted from him regardless, though her pussy flexed and rippled erratically around him as her body ached for something only her lover could provide.

If she'd been alone, masturbation would never have cut it. She needed him and arched her back, shoving her shoulder blades down into the bed, which squeaked lightly under their combined weight. The sheets would be made up later that day by housekeeping, but, for the moment, they rumpled and twisted almost uncomfortably under her back. It would have put her off if she hadn't been as worked up as she was, grunting and moaning as she tried to get more pleasure than ever. Rocking and grinding against her partner, she clung to his shoulders, burying her face in the uppermost part of his chest.

"Ah, yes… Dylan…" She moaned. "Harder! Harder, please!"

The dolphin clicked as he thrust, his tail swinging out behind him, though he couldn't curl it down against her. Poppy took care of that for him as she curled her tail around his as much as she could, though her tail was not flexible enough to wrap around him several times. The touch still brought them closer together, however, physical contact of the utmost importance to them.

It was not bad to be close, not even as Dylan thrust more roughly, allowing himself to give her everything she needed. He didn't want to be too crass with his lover, but the leopard just seemed to draw that out of him, thrust after thrust, stroke after stroke. Her pussy pulled around him as if she was doing it all deliberately and the ripple of her sex around his cock made his head spin.

He longed for the moment, huffing and panting, though it was not typical for a dolphin. To have her bring that out of him was exhilarating and she groaned under him, quivering bodily.

He ran a hand up her body, returning to teasing her breasts. There was not too much he could do in that position, though he managed to drop to his left elbow so he could caress her nipples at the same time. He didn't have nipples like that but hers were a lot of fun to tease, letting his fingers graze the pert nubs, her flesh indenting softly under the more urgent press of his fingers.

Poppy moaned his name and Dylan thrust on, his cock spearing in her deeply. She squeezed the full length of his cock with every thrust, though it was impossible to know whether it was due to how tight her pussy simply was. She clung to him as if she didn't want to let go and even her longer nails pricked into his skin, treating him as if they were claws.

He would have liked that if she'd really had claws. Having her claws raking long, hot lines into his back would have been pretty hot, but it wasn't the moment for Dylan to raise that. He grunted and powered in more roughly, long thrusts claiming her pussy. For the feline had already claimed every last inch of him and he was glad of it.

Dylan wouldn't have wanted it any other way, no, not at all. He was right where he needed to be as his heart pounded and his blood sang. It felt like every vein in his body had become a current, carrying blood and more around his body to where it needed to be, all in interconnected system. His mind didn't like to stay on one track in the throes of passion and, already, his cock tightened, something pulling in his groin.

His balls were held internally, as they were for many other dolphins too, and he thrust harder, not worrying about smacking his nuts into her body. Dylan wasn't all that sure if that would have been a fair concern if he'd had externally held balls, though it was something he'd thought about a little too much. He liked how he could thrust like that, however, letting every roll of his body flow into her, thrusting deep: it felt like swimming.

And having sex with Poppy was more natural to the dolphin even than swimming as he crammed every inch of his cock into her, stretching her out around him. Yet the leopard clenched increasingly tightly around him, so much so it would have been difficult for him to thrust and keeping filling her if not for her slick arousal coating his entire length. She was so wet around him that he could have slipped out if he was not careful to stay inside her, for the dolphin didn't want to pop out.

He wanted to stay deep, cumming into her pussy over and over again. There was no condom to separate their bodies from that delicious tease of skin on skin, but she was on the pill anyway. It was good to know there was no risk as Dylan gave himself over completely and utterly to the moment, his fingers pinching her nipple with a sharper bite than usual.

Poppy howled, her cry raw as if it had been dredged up from deeper inside her than he had ever called such a feral cry before. Her legs tightened around him, dragging his cock forcibly all the way inside her and holding him there. The dolphin had not even needed to rub her clit that time, for his teasing toying with her tits had been more than enough for her. He filed that little discovery away for later perusal, if her tits were so sensitive she could be pushed into orgasm from a rougher tease from time to time.

To play with them further was not for them in the moment, however, not as she cried out his name and brokenly rocked on his member. Dylan gave the leopard what she wanted with every stroke, her pussy pulling and twitching around him with every humping thrust. He needed his high too, even as liquid joy coated his cock.

And she cried out for him, clinging to him ruthlessly. He couldn't hold back, no longer stopping his thoughts from focusing on her as she was, how her breasts rubbed against his chest as he bore down even more on her, forced to relinquish her tit from his hold. It was a small price to pay for the closeness to come that morning, his cock driving deep until, at last, the dolphin could hold back no more.

He spent himself inside her with a deep, guttural groan that dragged at his throat as he released it. Yet that was nothing compared to the release of orgasm, powerful spurts of cum painting her pussy. His orgasms were typically strong, something that had come through from his aquatic ancestry, needing to drive his seed as deep as was possible to ensure the best chance of impregnation. It was not something he had to worry about anymore, though it meant his climaxes were typically messy when his cum was spent.

It dribbled around the length of his cock, offering another warm nuance to the friction, and his tail hung heavily. Energy left his body as his head went blissfully blank, nothing more than a creature of sensation. His cream bubbled with her arousal around the base of his shaft, where their bodies joined, and he stammered there, beak clicking as Dylan fought for words that simply would not come.

He didn't need to speak, however. Poppy swept her paws smoothly down his back, soothing him and settling him in the moment, allowing him to come back to her despite the heady rush of pleasure. Dylan blinked and moaned, shuddering as he was back in his full senses, his cock still buried in her hot, twitching pussy. The feline moaned luxuriously and rocked her hips up against him, careful not to put too much pressure on his lower back from where her legs hooked around him.

Yet he stayed there, his cock buried deep, letting every last drop of his seed flow into her. It was all they needed, all they longed for, huffing and panting lightly, together in the moment.

It was only morning, but it didn't look like there were going to get all that far out of the hotel room that day – and that was okay. They didn't have to do anything they didn't want to on that weekend trip together, enjoying one another at the coast.

A morning drifted into the afternoon and then the evening, swapping positions and pausing for sustenance: the perfect reconnection.

A Night of Pleasure

"Ah… Darling, I've been waiting for you."

Holly relaxed back, one leg crossed over the other, though the husky wasn't trying to hide anything at all. In her sitting room – for she had the luxury of having multiple reception rooms in her comfortable home – she had decked the room out in rich, red-tone furnishings. When she'd set it up and decorated, she'd wanted a den of luxury where she could relax and savour her evenings.

The grey-furred husky, after all, had spent more than enough time working hard in her life already. Now that she was where she wanted to be with a high-paying job that did not tax her as greatly as roles earlier in her career, she wanted to make the most of it. She had to live her life as she wanted, of course, and not fall prey to what others thought she could or could not do.

Her partner, thankfully, more than understood that – though there were more reasons than that as to why Holly had fallen for the tall dragon. Cecil grinned widely, though there was a heat in his cheeks that Holly could not fail to notice, even through his scales. In fact, it was only how his scales were a lighter blue, like the washed-out shade of the sky after a rainstorm in summer, which allowed such heat to show through his scales in the first place.

Holly hummed happily, her tail lifting slightly in that typical husky-like curl. Of course, Cecil's eyes could not help but linger on her body, one leg crossed over the other as she reached for a glass of red wine on the side table and took a sip from it. She didn't drink red all that often, though she'd found a vintage she simply had not been able to resist.

Dressed in some of her favourite lingerie, the pull of her heavy breasts was well shown off in the cups of her bra. Most of her cleavage was on show with her nipples comfortably covered, though her breasts were so large than many more conservative sorts would have said she was indecent even when she was fully covered anyway. That was why Holly resolved to live her life in the way she wanted to, caring not about what anyone else thought of her.

Someone was going to have an opinion, after all, with her slim waist and wide hips, her body shaped into the perfect hourglass. Holly had not even had to go to the gym all that much to gain such a figure, though she enjoyed the look when she developed her muscle lightly though. The husky was the type to build hard, lean muscle that shaped her body, though her older sister had gained more defined, larger muscle more easily than her. Every anthro was different, even when they came from the same family.

Holly had never lost the soft layer of flesh covering her buttocks and thighs, however, even if it was the muscle beneath it that gave her body such a sultry definition. Cecil had spent many hours down on his knees worshipping every inch of her body, dragging his tongue over exposed flesh between her thighs and kissing every inch of her. If Holly had not thought she deserved to be adored before, the dragon most certainly made sure she knew it every day.

I'm lucky to have him.

She grinned, though the dragon would not know what she was thinking as she set her leg back down from where it had been crossed over the other. The canine pushed her knees out slightly.

And he's lucky to have me too.

The dragon came in close and dropped to one knee before her, Holly letting out a delighted giggle as he raised her paw, kissing the back of it.

"Oh, you are always a gentlefur, aren't you, Cecil?"

"When you greet me like this, darling," he murmured, "how could I not be?"

The drake matched her nicely, though that was not why they had fallen for one another. His blue scales gave a hint of his heritage as a water dragon, though it would take going back several generations in his ancestry to find out exactly which ones had been an aquatic species. There was still a light, soft frill around the back of his jaw, though it was too small for him to really sense changes in the water when he was in it: merely a memento of times long gone by for his line of dragons.

There were two moderate horns, pointing straight back, on his skull too, his brows more heavily ridged with thicker, chunkier scales, which were presented around his raised nostrils too. If he'd been underwater, both his eyes and nostrils could have protruded above the surface, allowing him to see and breathe while hiding the majority of his body from prying eyes.

The rest of his body was more akin to a typical anthro with those pale scales spreading down his chest to his crotch while deeper, richer blue hues covered his shoulders, down his back, across his buttocks and around to his hips too. Most that darker blue, of course, could only be seen when he was out of his clothes – like the slender, pliable fin that ran down his back, starting at the point between his shoulder blades and slimming down close to the very tip of his tail.

Like most dragons, he had claws too, which was one way in which he differed from Holly; she had nails, kept painted more often than not. Yet clawed anthros kept them filed shorter and blunter usually, because it was considered the social norm. Catching them in fabrics and causing damage with them too was problematic if an anthro didn't take good care of them.

His chest was delightfully broad and Holly let out an appreciative murmur as he unbuttoned his striped work shirt to expose it. He didn't need to hide himself in any way, no, and Cecil was quite correct in assuming just how his evening was going to progress with his partner, even though Holly had a dinner planned for just the two of them too.

"Mm, I love seeing you like this," she breathed, running the flats of her paws down his chest, her fingers splayed out as if she was trying to cover as much of his chest as possible, even if she could not spread them across the whole span of it. "And there I was thinking you were going to work late tonight and keep me here waiting."

"Never, my darling."

Cecil chuckled throatily, though the drake didn't want to slip out of his black trousers just yet. One of his paws toyed with his belt, as if he was going to tug it free, though he set aside the notion for the moment.

The dragon wanted more to please his queen right then and there, gently spreading her legs a little more for him as he nuzzled up her inner thigh to the treat of her pussy. It was a forward motion but where was the sense in beating around the bush when Holly had already made her intentions clear?

He loved that about her. He never had to wonder or guess – unless it was all in good fun – what was going on with her. Sometimes it could throw other furs off, with how forward she was about how she was feeling and what she thought, but she was never rude about things like that either. Still, it could give others pause, for it was not usual for furs to be like that in their society.

But he loved it and he loved how she eased her legs apart for him, allowing him to kiss up from the inside of her knee to the light crease between her crotch and her thigh. It was light and covered with fur, though it was there. Her underwear was lightly laced with a silky body to it, not covering all that much at all.

It didn't need to as he took his time with her, rubbing his paws up and down her thighs, the long, soothing strokes of his paws rolling through her. Holly's breath caught and Cecil groaned lightly, pressing on, his lips brushing over the folds of her pussy through the fabric of her underwear.

"Oh…" She breathed. "That's what I like, darling."

Cecil always took such good care of her and the husky struggled not to roll her hips forward against him as she draped a leg sensually over his shoulder. She didn't need to draw him in against her or keep him there, though it was nice to warm her body up even more for their mutual pleasure.

He looked good like that, down on his knees, though the dragon had even more ways to make her moan for him. Last time they'd had sex, he'd pushed her knees back to her chest, allowing him to go deeper than ever inside her, using every inch of his ridged cock to plough into her. The long, devout strokes, as if every thrust was in an act of praise for her, had made her howl time after time again, reaching three orgasms from his shaft alone.

What could the husky say? He just had a way of always delivering exactly what she needed, even if Holly didn't know quite what she wanted.

"Mmm…"

She hummed happily, her tail wagging as he ran his tongue up her folds lightly, tasting her through the fabric.

"You're already wet, honey."

Holly chuckled throatily, trailing her fingers around the base of his horns. The dragon shivered under her touch.

"When am I not, for you?"

He murmured against her, pulling her panties to the side, though the dragon didn't want to reveal her completely, not quite yet. Not when that shared heat simmered beneath their fur and scales, prickling with longing. The drake grunted softly into the heat of her pussy, pushing into her sex and dragging up inside her. The long, slow lap of Cecil's tongue tickled her G-spot, though she only got a moment in which to buck her hips, his tongue swiping up to her clit.

Holly's moans rose and her toes curled as she clung to his short horns, losing herself, however briefly, to seductive need. She could let go, well and truly, with her partner, forgetting everything as he took her away to another place and time, her muscles trembling softly, releasing drops of tension. And yet there still had to be some manner of contraction in her body as she rolled her hips up to meet him, groaning faintly, tail flicking, as he suckled on her clit.

The husky moaned, struggling to bear through it for a few seconds, for she was very sensitive. Some oral pleasures had to be worked up to and his lips were stronger than those of a mammalian anthro – well, at least in Holly's experience. Yet the husky panted heavily, fighting to keep her long, pink tongue from lolling out too much from her muzzle. If she was going to come undone before him, like a present to be opened, she would do it in orgasm.

So, she would hold out from him for just a little more as he slid her underwear down her legs, revealing her in all her glory. The tasteful, moderate lighting threw shadows across the wall from the side lamps, keeping the overhead lights, as always, off. She never had any need of them, though Holly was able to catch a tantalising glimpse of his bulge. The dragon didn't have a sheath like some anthros or a slit, his genitalia held externally, which suited the husky just fine. She loved having everything be just where she could get at in, not tucked away.

His need was easier to see too, swelling through the front of his black work trousers, though she'd have them off him soon enough. But there was not a further moment for ogling, however, as he turned her over on to her front, allowing her to stand and brace herself on the back of the sofa. If Holly needed to, she could drop a knee to the sofa also, to better steady herself.

"I'm going to make you moan so loudly for me…"

Cecil whispered huskily, though his voice was a little raspy from need. He could have paused for a drink of water, though he didn't feel like there was time to do so as his aching hard-on swelled. It fleshed up as thick and as full as it could in his trousers, his boxers holding it gently, but it was not the drake's focus in the moment.

He would have her soon, but there was more than enough time to relax together as he left his belt hanging loosely though did no more to remove his trousers. Cecil exhaled as he knelt behind her, just about tall enough to be on the same level as her round buttocks as she bent over for him.

It was the perfect position for him to lap up into her pussy, flicking inside and dragging his tongue over her G-spot with every lick, just to feel her quiver. She'd orgasm on his muzzle, soon enough, though Cecil had a little trick up his figurative sleeve to play on her first. All within the bounds of their personal sexual limits, course, but definitely something that was destined to make her sing for him.

The first the husky knew of his loving little trick was his finger pressing up to her tail hole. Her tail quivered, flicked up as high as it could go in its little curl, but he pressed on, sliding a digit easily into her twitching pucker. She moaned, ducking her head and putting a round into her back, simply wanting to grind back on to his finger and tongue. Her head swam with delight and she bucked her hips like she was going to orgasm right then and there, though Holly wanted a little more pleasure from him beforehand, even if there was plenty more to come after her first orgasm.

Was it wrong of her to want to take advantage of every moment like that? The husky would never have thought so, not as she moaned and quivered, dropping that single knee to the sofa just so she could push back a little more. She had to use what leverage she had, rocking her hips, though she was under her lover's command in that moment.

"Mmph, ah…" She groaned. "Cecil…"

The dragon didn't have any words to spare as he lapped deeply up into her, his tongue catching and savouring her arousal with every stroke. She was so wet already that she made his heart pound, a driving beat in his chest that he had to follow the call of. The dragon pressed on, using the finger under her tail to work back and forth gently, though the husky opened up willingly around him.

There was no rush but, for her pleasure, he added a second finger, very slowly, stretching out her tail hole a little more. Her backside tightened around him for a moment before she relaxed and Cecil's heart leapt, his hard-on aching more than ever.

If only he could have risen right then and there to push her against the back of the sofa to take her. Oh, those feral needs and urges inside him were tantalising but not something he wanted to give in to, not when he could enjoy other pleasures with her. Maybe when they were both in the mood for something rougher, that was something they could talk about another time?

He'd see about it, though he lost himself as he lapped in deeply, his other paw coming up between her legs for the lightest stimulation of her clit. He could have brought her over the edge in a few moments but drew it out so her orgasm would be as strong as he could make it, while still feeding her need. His sweet husky moaned and grunted, her arms quivering where she had braced herself against the back of the sofa.

"Mmm... Ah, Cecil... I'm close!"

The last words came out almost as if in a bark, sharper than she most likely intended, though he was happy to bring her there and hungry to hear her sing.

His fingers inside her felt a lot bigger than they actually were, stimulating her in all the right ways as he thrust them gently within her ass. She squeezed around him, a whine on her lips, but Holly didn't pause as she let go a little more, the weight of her breasts swinging heavily in her bra as she shifted to contain the pleasure. It mounted, increasingly, though it came through as her legs shuddered, tail twitching from the root.

She didn't have to hold back, however, as every delicious line of tension in her body came to a peak at once, groaning and panting heavily through the sheer bliss of climax. She lost herself, if only for a time, yet rested secure in the knowledge that she was in her partner's paws, that she could rely on him to look after her, even if it would only be needed for a short time.

Her body sang, heat flooding her, and her moans simmered down, even as her pussy and anal passage clenched around both his tongue and fingers. Cecil was there to carry her through it, letting her ride out every moment the best he could, though his hard-on ached for attention too.

Holly would have been amiss if she ignored it, after all. His fingers withdrew from her tail hole, her pucker left slightly, minutely gaping for a moment before her body tightened up naturally again. Yet she couldn't help but turn around quickly, even if her legs shook lightly, clinging to his shoulders simply to drag the drake's lips to hers in a hungry kiss.

"Mmmph!"

Cecil grunted into the kiss, though his arms were around the husky in an instant, even though she was kneeling up on the sofa and at a higher level than him. For a moment, it left the dragon feeling smaller than he was, panting heavily into the kiss, her arms around his neck and shoulders to hold him against her.

In the kiss, their tongues tangled, sweeping hungrily up against one another, for Holly's desire had only been fed and not sated by that first orgasm. No, the husky was desperate for more, to feel more even as her breasts pressed up against him, his head tipped all the way up for their lips to meet at a somewhat comfortable angle. Her lips vibrated very faintly as she groaned into their passionate embrace, sharing joy as much as lust and, of course, love. For there was always going to be love there, at the heart of everything they took on together.

"Mm, please, Cecil," she breathed, breaking the kiss even if a string of saliva connected their lips for a moment. "I need you inside me. Though what you just did… That was amazing too."

She groaned as he hoisted her up on to the sofa and stood back.

"I think I can do that for you," he said, a cheeky grin tugging at his lips. "I was getting worried I was going to leak through my trousers too, heh."

She laughed lightly along with him, putting her arms back and up behind her head, crossing at the wrists. It was good to arch her back, pushing her chest forward, though spared a moment from the position to twist and unclasp her bra at the back too, sliding it from her shoulders. The dragon's eyes followed the path of her fingers as her breasts were revealed, full and heavy, tipped with pink nipples. Yet he had to focus on getting rid of his own clothes as he fumbled to make sure his belt wasn't catching, shoving his trousers down without ceremony.

His thick thighs were revealed, muscled nicely, and the swell of his calves outstripped hers by far. The drake had got into running at one point and working out was a little habit of his, done after work most days of the week. Not that day, of course, for Holly had asked to make sure he was heading home at the usual time, so she could plan her little surprise for him.

His boxer briefs tented out obviously with his shaft, though they'd done as good a job of restraining his cock as they could have hoped to. A large wet spot showed just where his pre-cum had already leaked through, though it was not as if the drake was going to worry all that much about a little thing like that. It was all by the by as he finally freed his aching erection, letting his hard shaft spring into the open air.

Even though it was normally smooth and fleshy when it was soft, every ridge popped up when he was hard, running up the full length of his shaft. The head had a more reptile-like definition to it, tapered to a point with the slit puckering as if ready for more, the glands defined. He ran his fingers around it, though found himself already hard and wanting, not needing any further preparation at all.

How fortunate that was…

"Mmm, come here, darling," she murmured, her voice taking on a lower, more seductive tone as she led the situation once again. "I need you now."

She lay back on the lounger section of the sofa, which was mostly used for stretching out their legs, her buttocks close to the end. It was a taller seat that their old sofa and kind of chosen for the fact it was easier for him to thrust into her when she was on all fours on it.

On her back, however, the challenge was increased as he let his knees bend and lined up with her pussy, his quads contracting to hold his body in place. Even his abdominal muscles had to pull in lightly to take care of his core, glutes tensing. Everything came into play in ways he never would have thought of in sex, though it was a workout he was more than merely passionate about.

As the drake leaned over her for a better angle, balancing on both paws beside her head, he rolled his hips smoothly forward, the tapered head of his cock catching in the folds of the husky's pussy. Her groan was music to his ears as he sank inside her and the only thing that could have possibly made the moment better would have been soft background music, just to add that extra touch of romance.

What could Cecil say, he was a bit of a romantic at heart. Or maybe his sweetie had merely brought out a side of him he had not, before, known existed.

Holly panted under him, her pink tongue flicking up against her lips and then sweeping back inside. It was delicious to sink into her when she was as wet as she was already, her pussy rippling and pulling erratically around him, though not in the same way it would when she was actually in the height of orgasm. Cecil grunted, letting the roll of his hips carry him deeper, yet the drake trembled. It did not feel like it was the moment to hold back, not anymore.

It was more the time to let passion carry him on, trusting in his husky to let him know what felt good and what did not, all so they could even better enjoy one another. Cecil groaned, thrusting deeper, drawing back only to drive in another couple of inches, until he was using the full length of his cock to fill her.

Her slick folds clung to him, almost sucking around his cock as he withdrew, though her legs raised and locked around his waist, holding him there. Holly ran her paws up his arms to his shoulders and upper back, though she didn't grip him tightly, resting there and languishing as she groaned aloud.

"Ah… Yes…"

Holly couldn't get out any more words than that – and she didn't have to either, not as her chest rose and fell in passion. She hadn't bothered to take the time to remove her jewellery, just a necklace and a bracelet, before getting into things and they caught the light with a subtle glint as the dragon's hips rolled. The drake's cock speared deeply into her and she bucked her hips up, using the leverage her legs had on his waist, taking control even though she was in the bottom position.

There was no true top and bottom between them when the husky and the dragon were as used to swapping back and forth as they were. Holly's chest rose as she took a deeper, more juddering breath than before, yet the husky was right where she needed to be, letting the moment roll through her.

It didn't need to be anything more than what it was, the canine licking her lips as her tail tried to wag from even where it was trapped between her backside and the sofa. She moaned softly, squeezing her thighs around him, though she could always trust her drake to give her everything she needed.

"Mmm… Deeper…" She breathed. "You know I can take more than that."

"Always, love."

Cecil thrust harder, as she wished, though kept his strokes long and powerful, even if there was more force behind it. One benefit of the ridges on his cock was that they pulled and raked pleasantly over her clit with every thrust, grinding tenaciously. He groaned, the tight pull of her wet pussy around him hard to bear, but he didn't want to cum inside her too quickly.

Holly made that difficult for him, however, even as he grunted and groaned, a thinner, more slippery tongue flicking from his mouth and then drawing back in. The dragon grunted and hissed through his teeth, eyes filled with love and warmth for his partner. They never once left her face – okay, so maybe a few times they dropped to the bounce and sway of her breasts – and the gentle lines of her beautiful muzzle.

He preferred positions where they were facing one another, though Holly made her intentions for something more along those lines clear to him as she tightened her grip on his waist. Tipping to the side, she whined and pulled him with her, though Cecil went along with the push of her body so they, without separating, shuffled around. His arms went around the husky as he pulled her up against him and briefly, stood with her impaled on his member, turning to sit back down himself.

With her in his lap, they could truly be face to face as she rose and fell on his cock. The husky's knees nestled on either side of the dragon's body with his back against the pillows of the sofa.

Cecil groaned.

"Mmm... You know I love this position."

"Just as much as I do, honey."

She kissed him passionately, cupping his cheek tenderly in her paw. All it took was a rock of her hips to grind all the way down on her cock, positioning her hips in just the right position to tease her clit against one of his ridges. Everything came together, sweetly, as it needed to and she moaned into his mouth as her hips rose and fell increasingly urgently.

Cecil tensed his abs, using that light rock of his pelvis to add to her thrusts, though they were both close already. There was no need to rush the moment as they panted hotly into one another's muzzles and swapped sides, tipping their muzzles the other way to better lock their lips together. Her tail wagged fervently, finally free to do so, and Cecil grunted into her mouth, shuddering under her while she tightened her grip on him.

Together, they climaxed, though it was a sweet spill over the edge, feeling it coming in the last few pumps before it actually hit. Her lower stomach pulled, tension rising through her body, yet the husky was willing to let it come, desire flowing hotly through, filling her body from the bottom up. Cecil tucked his muzzle down slightly, even though he didn't want to break the kiss, his tail curling around Holly's ankle, just for that added touch and closeness.

He didn't want to lose himself, even as his nuts ached and need surged inside him. It was not to be held back as he savoured the moment with her and she was forced to break the kiss in ragged moan. Holly's head fell back as Cecil nipped at her neck, letting her lose herself in orgasm while her sex tugged around him. The clench and pull of muscles was not something the husky could control, in the heat of the moment, but it dragged them along as if their lust in itself was not something they could restrain at such a time.

And it was as it was meant to be as they groaned and moaned together, Cecil's sharp teeth raking pleasantly down her neck as desire carried them through. He thrust harder, tipping into orgasm just like his sweet husky, and spent his seed inside her. Long, thick spurts of seed, over productive as always, flooded her pussy, a little cum bubbling and drooling out the join between their bodies.

Yet he was too lost in pleasure to care about the mess they were making in the course of their lovemaking, panting heavily, shuddering with every pump. Together, they took their pleasure, wrapped up in one another's arms, as close as it was possible to be. Grinding down all the way on to his cock, Holly panted heavily, not caring any longer that her tongue was spilling out, her lips stretched into a wide, almost goofy grin. Cecil, of course, would never have pointed that out to her. He loved when she let go.

There was nowhere else either would have wanted to be as they rested their foreheads together, tenderly sharing the moment while his aching hard-on remained deep inside her. They breathed deeply, though perhaps not evenly while they settled again, a throbbing sense of fullness aching through Holly.

A night of pleasure, even beyond that, awaited them. And they were more than ready to rest, refuel and see just where the evening, and wine, took them.

Together, they could do no wrong.

Deepthroat

The red wolf's tail swung back and forth lightly, just a few inches, though she kept it loose and relaxed, licking her lips lustfully. Dressed in some of her finest lingerie, she'd bought it especially for that night with her partner, Nook. They were home, in their bedroom, but she'd made sure everything was extra nice for her Dalmatian partner, the canine who she'd been with for three years already.

It felt like a lifetime they'd been together, but Dalia knew there was so much more left to come between them. They had not yet lived every last one of their years together and the prospect of getting to live and love so much more with Nook made her heart leap, tightening in her chest as it pounded.

There was so much left to experience… And Dalia was there for that moment.

In her black lingerie with the tiny gems inset into the fabric, her breasts certainly looked their best, her cleavage lightly defined and the cups of her bra perfectly moulded around the soft flesh there. Nook would have said her breasts looked perfect at all times, although the canine was often more interested in other things. Like adoring her body from head to toe, kissing her all over, letting the red wolf know exactly how much he loved her.

"Did you wear this just for me?" Nook murmured, though the dog already knew the answer. "You don't always have to get this dressed up, just for me. Though I love seeing you like this."

The red wolf smiled and parted her knees where she sat on the very edge of the bed, inviting him closer. Nook grunted in the back of his throat and shuffled in, his shirt already unbuttoned and his tie cast aside after going out with Dalia that evening. His shaft throbbed in his pants, though he'd worn black suit trousers that time, for they were better suited to the location they had been out to.

They didn't often see the need for fine dining when they preferred simpler comforts and joy, like curling up before a fireplace or even going camping in the wilderness together. But it was good to experience all they could in life too, leaving nothing untouched and no stone unturned. If sitting across a table with a white linen tablecloth with fine wine and the best of company was to be experienced, he wanted everything of it – all with Dalia.

"Always for you, darling," the wolfess all but purred, even though Dalia didn't have any feline ancestors at all – not that she knew of, at least. "I want to look my best for you. But I actually have something very special in mind tonight."

The Dalmatian's ears picked up, twitching, though they were lightly folded over and sometimes did not have quite as much movement in them as those of other canines. There was something about the muscles and nerves at the base of his right ear too that prevented it from moving as much as it could have, although Dalia had not even noticed it until Nook had once pointed it out to her. That had been back in the early days of them dating.

"What did you have in mind?"

Nook was quick to ask and she drew him up on to the bed with her heart pounding, need coursing through her. The wolf barely even kept it under the surface as her tail lifted excitedly, turning around and sliding back off the bed as she asked him to take her previous position. The canine let out a soft grunt, blinking a little more, but did as she quietly asked of him. It was usually Dalia who led, sexually, in their relationship, but they were more likely to pass organisation and control of things outside the bedroom back and forth between them otherwise.

He didn't mind that, not one bit. Not as she slid his shirt expertly back from his shoulders and exposed every last one of his black spots on his upper half. His chest was nicely broad – but not too wide for her either. She wanted still to be able to get her arms around him, to not feel like she was dwarfed by him. Dalia was sure she would have fallen head over heels for the canine anthro, however, regardless of how he looked. That sort of thing didn't matter to the wolf, yet she still appreciated him for what he was and how he was.

The Dalmatian's breath hitched and he squirmed as she pulled down his black trousers, undoing his belt with a deft flick of her fingers. The wolf was so smooth about everything she did and he wished he could maintain that same level of composure in himself, breathing slowly and evenly despite everything. He wanted to be there in the moment, to savour everything.

From the slide of her fingers across his thigh as she worked his trousers down further.

The glint in her eye as she caught his gaze – then looked away once more.

How her tail lifted, drawing his eye in that bristle of red fur.

The scent of her need marked the air, something not even the wolfess could hide. He doubted Dalia would ever have tried to hide it.

"Ah… Oh, Dalia…"

He moaned and tipped his head back as she pulled his trousers all the way down and took care of his boxer briefs too. There was a wet spot at the front, marking his bulge, and he grunted as she freed his erection, letting the hard length of dog cock spring out. The tip was already slick, even if he'd rubbed a little pre-cum off on his undergarments, the head tapered to a smooth point. Yet the girth was hard and ran down to an unformed knot at the base, his cock fully out of his sheath.

"I know how to take good care of you, darling," Dalia said. "So, let me."

She phrased it as if he didn't have any choice in the matter and, still, he wanted to go along with it, like a little puppy for her. Maybe they would venture into more domination and submission play in the future, see where that led them, but that was for another time.

Still, he loved when she was in charge and he loved when she put him in his place. Nook only wished Dalia was naked, that he could see even more of her in that moment.

He would have to wait, however, for the moment was about the wolfess and what she wanted to do to him.

Dalia sank into it, licking her lips. Her fingers casually slid around the base of his cock, down to where the sheath covered the very bottom of his length. That part of him would always be hidden from her, no matter how much she ground down on to his cock, forcing his sheath to crinkle back and expose another little sliver of his shaft.

His groan encouraged her on and he rolled his hips forward a little as she nuzzled at his cock. She avoided getting his pre-cum on her fur, for that wasn't something Dalia particularly enjoyed, but lapped up the length of his cock, from the base to the tip.

The long, flexible length of her tongue stroked up his cock, flicking around the head and scooping his pre-cum into her mouth. It was only a tiny bubble there, nothing more than a smear, yet she grunted lightly, savouring it. It was a lot, so very carnal, and one of the most intimate things she felt she could do for him.

Dalia pressed her lips around the head of his cock, lapping gently and swirling her tongue around as if she truly had all the time in the world for him. It was easy for her to sink into it, working his cock with one paw, her fingers folded sensually around his length while her lips teased the tip. She didn't want to get him going too swiftly, drawing out the pleasure bit by bit and moment by moment, for it was the she-wolf's game to play. And Dalia was going to play every single second out just as she wanted.

Dalia murmured around his cock, a little ripple going through her as her partner twitched and fidgeted under her. Oh, she loved when she got him going like that, as if he couldn't think about anything other than her, struggling more than Nook clearly wanted to admit from all she was doing to him. Such small touches and teases should never have had as big an effect on a fur as they did – yet they persevered. That was the beauty of a partner, the intimacy that could be explored in sex.

The little things grew loud. It was in those moments they mattered the most.

So, she took the time, even if she could have got him off right then and there, letting him feel everything. Her tongue pushed down the length of his cock as her lips descended. Dalia took Nook's throbbing length deep into her maw with tantalising slowness – so slowly that it was as if she was never going to reach the bottom. He grunted and squirmed but never pressured her to go quicker, his eyes locked on her.

She could feel it. The intensity of his stare bore through her, digging under even her skin. Yet Dalia was always right where she wanted to be as she quivered bodily, a ripple running through her, from her head to the very tip of her tail. The wolfess' tail flicked and she moaned around his shaft, drooling ever so slightly. Not everything, when it came to sex, could be kept clean and pristine. Sometimes, it was the messiest parts that were the most lustful too.

Dalia grunted faintly, though the wolf didn't lose herself there. No, she was completely in control of herself as she bobbed her head, so very slowly, on his length. Suckling around his cock, she drew the tip of his cock into the back of her throat and held him there, doing no more than that.

Before her, Nook squirmed and panted.

"Agh… Dalia, you're teasing me."

She was, indeed, though she wasn't about to stop to waste words when she had his cock in her mouth. Oh, no, her dog was going to have to wait and enjoy the suckle of her lips pulling and twitching around his cock first. It would have been too nice of her, of course, for the wolf to draw the Dalmatian sweetly over the edge without asking for something first. And that "something" was his trust in her.

Nook trusted that she would bring him off when she was ready, that his wolfess would not make him wait and wait and wait while he squirmed and whined. The canine's paws fluttered around her head, as if he didn't want to rest them on her hair or her head. Her hair was trimmed shorter, coming down past her cheeks but not brushing her shoulders, but Dalia didn't mind him mussing it up. It was almost a badge of honour to finish sex with her fur all ruffled in the right places, rocking her hips back and forth.

She barely even realised how hot and bothered she was getting, pausing at the head of his cock to play her tongue over the tip. There were so many sensitive nerve endings up there that she could have spent all day on the head of his shaft, running her tongue over the slit and dipping, sweetly, inside. It was only a flutter of a touch, for she could not penetrate his shaft with her tongue, though the quivers running through him were delicious.

It was why she enjoyed giving him head as much as she did. And Nook knew it too as he grunted and lapped at her cock, hissing softly through his teeth as he struggled to remain in place.

The canine's paws landed on her at last, one on the back of her neck and the other wound through the strands of her hair, digging in lightly. Yet Nook would not force her to do anything, his tail trying to wag even where he was half-sitting on it, the bed squeaking under the weight of his body.

"Oh, Dalia… Yes…" He moaned, tongue lolling haplessly from his mouth as Nook shuddered bodily. "Yes… You know exactly what you do to me, you're amazing, you're wonderful, you're beautiful… Oh, your *tongue*!"

He half-yelped, struggling to vocalise his cries. There was no reason at all for Nook to be quiet, yet it already felt like his cock was going to explode. Kind of in the good way and kind of in the bad way too, for a few rough thrusts and he could have spent his slick load straight down her throat with no trouble at all. But that was not the deal of the moment as his cock pulsed within her mouth, the cradle of her tongue hypnotic.

It was funny, even to the Dalmatian, just how things like that played out. It was intoxicating and he allowed himself a roll of his hips, soft and subtle. The canine didn't need to do any more than that as he grunted in the back of his throat, blinking up at the soft lighting of the bedroom. Everything was familiar and yet, somehow, Dalia made it all feel simply electric, as if sparks were coursing through his veins in lieu of blood.

He moaned and tried to pull his tongue back into his mouth, licking his lips, though she deep throated him again. His fingers eased to the side of her neck, yet the canine could not quite feel the bulge of his cock there. Nook didn't want to press down on her throat, after all, and make her gag – she already had more than enough to take into her mouth. His cock was large but not too large, so she could deep throat him.

A long, low moan escaped him as her throat pulled around the head of his cock. She bobbed back and forth, sometimes lingering deeply and other times letting her tongue swipe around and toy with the head of his shaft. She kept him guessing, moment by moment, and he moaned, barely even knowing what to do with himself as his toes curled. There was nothing for them to dig into, for his partner had been swift enough to swipe off his socks too.

That was good. Nook hated having sex with socks on. Not that the canine would have turned down sex, however, just because he was wearing socks.

His head swam pleasantly and he looked down, eyes watering with the strain of keeping himself held back and in place. The bedroom took on an otherworldly quality, as if it was not just their bedroom but a more sensual space too, one they could only reach when they were together. He panted heavily and tried to rock up into her mouth, although the wolf had him right where she wanted him already, pinning him down lightly with a touch on his thigh. All it took was that touch to keep him in place.

Nook knew the limits. He grunted and licked his lips, though his peak was coming. She would have him and he leaned desperately into the moment as she pulled back, only to work her paw around his cock, teasing him to another treat of sensation.

"Mmm, are you ready, love?" She breathed, her breath tickling the tip of his cock. "I could have you here, but you're going to be mine, all mine, for the rest of the night."

His heart leapt, thudding almost painfully in his chest.

"Oh, anything for you, darling," he moaned back at her, his words barely understandable through his grunts and pants. "I want...anything you want. Everything... Mmm!"

He moaned, barely with himself in the moment, but that was alright. Dalia would carry him through and the wolf did just that.

Taking control, she stroked his cock, squeezing the growing knot as it plumped up against her paw. She tightened her grip as if she was trying to force his knot back down, though, of course, the wolfess would never have truly wanted that. She just yearned to bring him to that edge again – and finally let him tumble over into his high.

It was not up to him, after all. She dragged her tongue luxuriously around his cock, curling it around as much of the length as she was able. Dalia groaned softly, letting the subtle vibrations tremble into his cock, though it was merely an afterthought to the greater pull of pleasure. His cock tangibly throbbed within her mouth as she took him deep, roughly and crudely bobbing her head. Her tongue swept along the underside with every stroke, mimicking how he may have thrust, yet she had all she needed in the moment.

At least, until he howled brokenly and exploded in a raw and ragged climax. Long shots of cum spurted from his cock, marking her mouth and some going straight down her throat. She swallowed hard, suppressing her gag reflex the best she could, keeping his cock as deep inside her muzzle as she could at all times. It would have simply been a shame to pull back and let any of his seed be wasted, after all, and her heart filled with warmth at hearing her lover moan like that.

Whether she was on top or on the bottom, there was nowhere else Dalia would have rather been other than with him. She took his seed down her throat, pressing deeper, and exhaled through her nose, relaxing there.

In deep throating him, she'd taken an intimate part of him and, once again, shown the Dalmatian he could trust her. There was still plenty more of their night together to come, but the wolf was determined to enjoy the moment.

He moaned above her and she rubbed his thigh soothingly. He could rest there for as long as he needed, his tail wagging and twitching against the bed, rustling against the sheets. Yet Dalia murmured around him again, even her tail lifting and wagging, very faintly, back and forth.

No words were spent, not yet, as they relaxed there, exhaling as she pulled back from his cock, releasing her grip on his hard, swollen knot. It would take some time for that to deflate, though Dalia was in no rush.

Never with him. Not with Nook.

His fingers slid around to her neck and he drew her to him for a kiss, the wolf nestling into his arms as her heart soared. The taste of his cum still lingered in her mouth, although Nook wasn't bothered by that.

Together, they lusted. Together, they loved.

Together, they had every last moment of their life together to live and enjoy.

Soft Lust

Emily giggled and cradled her lover's head to her chest as she sprawled out on the bed in the hotel room. The cat's veins were still pleasantly warm and tingling after the wine they'd shared at dinner, although perhaps the two of them had imbued a little too much of it. Her long tail flicked back and forth in that inherently feline fashion, as if there was always something on her mind, something she was trying to hunt down.

Her shirt pushed down, revealing her blue-grey fur and a little of her heritage from a family of Russian blue cats – but anthros could be with whoever they liked those days, thankfully. It meant it was often a surprise how their offspring turned out, whether they took after the father or the mother or were a hybrid of both. Sometimes even surprising twists in their genetics popped up too – and that was without even looking at using a sperm bank and donor!

However, the feline was quite happy right where she was, her dhole partner nuzzling up to her neck. Hai's nose brushed into the crook of her neck and she purred happily, her chest rumbling under his cheek.

"Mmm, I love when you're like this..." He breathed, the wild dog pressing in closer. "Sweetheart... Do you know how beautiful you even are?"

"Oh, stop it, you!"

She laughed and tried to push him off, though Emily didn't really want him to stop. She loved how Hai brought a blush to her cheeks, even if it was mostly hidden under her fur. She just didn't mesh with anyone else as well as she did with the dhole and he was her best friend in the whole world too.

Going out with him had been much needed. In the busy rush of life, she just didn't feel they got to spend as much quality time together as they had before. They lived together, yes, but there was always something to do, someone to buy a gift for – oh, and that "thing" they forgot to get organised too! So, she was always wrapped up struggling and straining to keep up with seemingly everything in her life and the world all at once, perhaps even taking on more than Emily needed to.

That was okay, however: purely as Emily had Hai there to ground her. As he rolled on to his back under her, coaxing the feline up on top of his stomach, her blue-grey tail swished back and forth.

Emily's knee nudged between his legs and she grunted in the back of her throat, lightly. She wanted to be close to him, so very much so, and that delicious lick of heat inside her pooled at her core. They'd been out to see a show earlier too, on stage, and she should have been a lot more tired than she was, but all the cat could think about was her lover.

She purred more deeply as she stroked down his chest, tugging at the buttons on his shirt, playing with them. Yet his paws swept down her back, tracing the line of her spine, as they found a place to rest at the base of her back, right at the top of her glutes.

"Ah… Darling," she breathed, hardly daring to raise her voice anymore. "How do you make the smallest things feel so good? I wish I knew…"

"Hm…" He pretended to ponder the question for a moment, though the dhole's cheeky grin told the feline otherwise. "I don't know… Maybe I just get lucky?"

He didn't have to pull out quirky quips to keep her interested and sometimes it was the simplest of things that had her heart doing somersaults. The feline pushed up, tail flicking, though her eyes smouldered as they locked on to Hai's.

"Maybe you're very lucky, darling," she said, sliding off him and half-turning, stretching to pull off her top over her head. "To have me… To be with me… Don't you think so?"

When she met his eyes again, there was a new sense of hunger there and he licked his lips, letting out a needy whimper as he gulped. It came out a little strangled, but Emily managed to stop herself from giggling, for she didn't want to put the dog off.

No… He scared easy, as sweet as he was. And all she wanted to do was to be soft with him, at least that time.

She slipped back up on to the bed with him – and from that point on it was difficult to tell where one of them ended and the other began. She moaned as his lips tickled her neck, nipping and teasing in gentle caresses; he used his teeth too, catching lightly, but never hard enough to hurt her.

It was light and it was soft and it was everything she needed in the moment as she curled around him. Their paws roamed one another's bodies as they explored and tugged their clothes free, slowly but surely stripping one another nude. She panted heavily as he nuzzled into her bare breasts, the bra half trapped under her back – but the feline didn't care. She didn't care one bit as he nuzzled into her and lipped at her nipples, catching them very lightly and gently between his teeth.

"Ah, honey," Emily moaned. "You know what that does to me!"

She squirmed under his touch, although Hai's muzzle was rather busy at that moment. The dhole still had one sock on, somehow, but they were otherwise both nude. It didn't matter that things were a little messier, only that they were there. As he suckled on her nipple, Emily arched her back up towards him, her chest pushing increasingly urgently into his muzzle. Yet that was just her need coming to the forefront of her mind, snapping and snarling, trying to drive her on to passion.

Yet times could be slow and patient in that moment too. She whimpered faintly, letting him suckle on first one nipple and then the other. Hai's tongue swept and curled around her left nipple sensually, sucking it up between his lips. A broken cry rose from her muzzle as her lips parted, head falling back against the pillows.

He didn't let up, not in the slightest. He squeezed the breast he didn't have tucked between his lips, running his fingers over her nipple and teasing. For Hai more than knew where all those sensitive nerve endings were in her body and she groaned deeply in the back of her throat, lips twitching and pulling over her teeth.

The feline's body tried to say she had to fight, had to take what her body needed – yet it was Emily's mind that confirmed, at least to her, that she had all the time in the world with her lover. It was lustful, yes, but there was love too, winding through every breath of their time together. It was all the rush that had separated them when all the couple had wanted was to be close together, to be able to take that time with one another that there simply had not been.

Together, they could reconnect. Always together.

She arched her hips up to him, her pussy wet with desire. It was impossible for her to hide her heat from his questing nose and he inhaled deeply as he broke from her breasts. Hai licked his lips, eyes gleaming, yet didn't spare a word as he nuzzled down the full length of her torso, slowly. He took his time, kissing her fur, yet the two of them were only just getting started.

Emily mewled helplessly as Hai's tongue flicked out against the edge of her pussy. He teased her labia where her fur was thinner, until his tongue slipped into the smooth touch of her folds. Her pussy ached for him and he grunted into her sex, lapping softly into her sex.

Hai's skilful tongue curled up inside her pussy, sweeping up against her inner walls, and her blood sang for him. There was nothing like Hai's tongue and she lost herself there, reaching back up and over her head to grip haphazardly on to the headboard of the bed. Her hips rocked lightly from one side to the other, but Emily didn't need to do anything. All she needed to do was to feel and to let the moment roll on around her, for they would both take care of one another that night.

With each other, they finally had time and space and he pressed his fingers tenderly into her thighs, spreading them apart. He huffed hotly into her pussy as if he was struggling to regulate his own breath, but the dhole was quite alright where he was. In fact, Hai would have said that was the best place for him, tucked between her thick, soft thighs, one of his paws resting up a little higher on the gentle pudge of her belly.

Emily didn't see that, however, nor the way he looked adoringly up the length of her body, as if the blue-grey feline was the most beautiful thing in the world to him. Yet the moment was about so much more than that as she moaned and rocked up, thrusting and grinding, losing control over herself.

Thankfully for the cat, she had her partner there with her to catch her as she fell, two of his fingers sliding into her pussy and dragging back out again. There were lots of things in oral play she liked, but it was his tongue first the feline desired. His wide, curling tongue pushed back into her pussy, dragging through her folds, and she cried out breathlessly, quivering.

Closer and closer to the edge, she grunted lightly and rolled her hips up; her legs trembled and Emily was barely able to support her own body quite like that. She didn't have to, yet her body hummed with delicious energy, the spiralling twists of need in her belly curling. There was only one way in which to release that and, with Hai, it would not take long at all.

She couldn't hold back as his tongue danced temptingly over her G-spot, flicking and teasing, even if perhaps she had been rather close to the edge already. Something about being with her lover put her in just the right mood for sex, her body aching from head to toe. Yet it was a good ache, the kind that pulled deliciously through her and made her feel like she was floating away. No longer could Emily be tethered to a mortal plain as her body sang with ecstasy, her pussy tightening and pulling around his tongue as if she was striving to draw it deeper into her body.

The feline was not in control, not at all, letting out a cat-like yowl as he held her down to the bed with a large paw, keeping her in place. It was all for the cat's pleasure, of course, as his eyes fell half-lidded, drinking up her arousal with every rush. The sweet moment wrapped around them, as if they truly were secluded away from the rest of the world in the hotel room, nothing else existing aside from them.

When Emily came down from her high, she panted heavily, chest heaving for breath. Her toes curled and she stretched luxuriously, whimpering as he tickled her sex with his tongue. She was sensitive, too sensitive, but the feline didn't have the energy to push him away – and neither did she want to. Even if she ached desperately and her body thrummed with an edge of strain, she was right where she needed to be.

Later, when she took his shaft into her mouth and showed him everything he meant to her, they would come together even more closely in softening, sweetening lust.

Like Bunnies

"Oh! You can't grab me while I've got a hot tray in my paws, be careful – careful, now!"

Honey giggled, her ears bouncing atop her head where they had been perked, her husband playfully hassling her while she put the hot tray back in the oven. The rabbit anthros had been married for three years and together for five, though it still felt like they were in the honeymoon phase of their relationship. Sure, they had their fights and all, but things were so good between them, perhaps as they had similar personalities.

Or maybe bunnies just got on well together, Honey with her golden-brown fur with a darker brown-grey smudge across the top of her nose, below her eyes, and Basil with his predominantly black coat. Honestly, even with her sensitive eyesight at night, it was tricky sometimes for Honey to see Basil if he was hiding his white paws and the drop of white on his chest too.

Basil laughed at her, dressed comfortably for the evening in loose pyjama bottoms and a loose dressing gown, though it was open at the front to expose his narrow chest. Mischief danced in the bunny's eyes, one of his ears a little floppier than the other, though no one had ever been able to tell quite how that was so with him. Basil, however, suspected an injury when he was much younger – so young that it had always been that way with him.

He let his wife go, however, admiring the curve of her hips in her skirt and comfortable top, though it dipped between her breasts to expose her cleavage. She had been working in the office that day, with casual wear, but wanted to bake something for his parents, as they were visiting family the next day.

"You're always working," he murmured, brushing her blonde hair back from her face, the fine little hairs there as flyaway as they always were. "You need to take a break, darling, put your feet up. Maybe I can get this out of the oven when it's done? Or make the icing for you?"

"Oh, sweetie, I know you want to be helpful, but I enjoy it! You know I do, you know."

Honey smiled, leaning back against the kitchen counter as her husband's arms framed her on either side, holding on lightly to the counter as he did so. The bunny shivered. Whereas she had long, wavy hair, he didn't have anything more than a black tuft of fur between his upright ears, which was usually quite unruly. It was just one thing that came up sometimes with anthros, some gaining additional hair to style on their heads while others remained softly in a more natural state.

He tipped her chin up so their lips brushed and there was no more natural way in which they could have come together, Honey giving a slight intake of breath in the moment before their lips touched. They kissed and her heart leapt, stimulating something deep inside her, even if her husband was rather good at getting her all hot and bothered in the best of ways.

"Mmm…"

Honey murmured softly into the kiss as her husband deepened it, their lips parting as their tongues brushed up gently against one another. Her heart pounded and she let it all happen, even if the bunny was not at all against what was happening.

"Oh, Basil," she giggled faintly, ever so slightly light-headed as they broke the kiss. "I wasn't expecting any of this at all."

The buck rabbit grinned, his black ears twitching, though he was quite confident where he was already, not minding in the slightest how his evening was going. It was just a shame he hadn't realised

Honey was so busy with baking earlier on in the evening – he would have helped!

Yet there were other ways he could get Honey to relax and picking her up to sit on the kitchen table, where they usually perched for breakfast and other quick meals. She squealed playfully as his fingers dug into the softness of her plumper thighs, though all was well and good between them. They knew just where one another's boundaries lay and would never cross them unduly, even if they could stop fun with each other whenever, if anything ever came up.

That security in a relationship, along with trust, was more important to both than even they had vocalised. It was simply inherent.

"Ah, Basil…"

Honey whimpered as his fingers slid up her thighs, pushing her long, flowing skirt out of the way as he revealed her golden legs. The skirt caught up over her hips and Honey gulped faintly as he nuzzled straight up into the dampness in the middle of her panties, where the lightest of damp spots was showing.

Yet she didn't want to stop anything, no, and parted her legs a little more for him – though not so much that the rabbit couldn't slide her panties down her legs. She was glad she'd worn one of her favourite pairs that day: pink with tiny carrots dotted all over them. Sure, they weren't the sexiest of pairs, even with the little bit of lace, but they framed her butt nicely and made her feel good. She didn't always have to be sexy – cute was fine for Honey too.

Basil let her skirt bunch up over his forehead, his wife's fingers stroking over his ears and through the thicker tuft of black fur between them, as he lapped into her pussy. Sure, it was a bit quick for how Basil usually liked to start things with his wife, but he didn't want to miss her timer when the buns in the oven were ready. She had even started on a batch of cookies too…

He'd help her with the rest of it, he vowed, even as his tongue confidently traced the outline of her folds, flicking up to drag over the rising nub of her clit. It peeked out from its hood, stealing his attention, and the bunny groaned in the back of his throat, whiskers quivering as he pressed on.

Honey, however, was there for every bit of attention he had for her, letting her husband so skilfully sweep away all those little niggles and tensions of the day. Maybe she'd known too what her husband would have her do if he thought she was working too hard, though Honey didn't mind that he looked after her just like that in the slightest.

It was just another little thing that made their relationship with one another work as well as it did.

So, she leaned back, curling her fingers around the edge of the table for a little more balance, taking a deep breath. It shuddered in her chest and she could barely breathe as she rocked her hips up lightly to his lips. Even then, the old, wooden table, solid, of course, groaned under the shift of their bodies, but Honey had no fear of it not holding their weight. It had before.

"Oh… Yes… Just like that," she whimpered, resting her paw delicately on his head, though she wanted to keep her other one on the table for stability. "Ah… Basil…"

She groaned and half-closed her eyes, losing her sense of self in the moment. With Basil, it felt like nothing other than the current moment existed, allowing her to truly be – whoever that was. It almost didn't matter what happened as he tested her readiness with first one finger and then a second pushing up into the velvety, wet heat of her pussy, for pleasure went paw in paw with all they experienced.

"Mmm… Basil, please, I need you…" She tried, though the words came out airily, as if they were struggling to make it out from her voice box. "The timer… It's going to go off."

"Ah, don't worry," he murmured, lips brushing her clit as his breath tickled her slicker folds. "I'll make sure we don't miss it. And we can do whatever you like for the rest of the evening, promise."

Honey murmured, heat rushing to her cheeks, though it was hidden by the golden brown of her fur. Her husband shrugged off his dressing gown as he stood again and pushed down his pyjama bottoms, revealing his growing shaft. He had a very small sheath, tucked up and plump, that was mostly hidden in the black fur at the base of his belly, but his cock swelled from it. The shaft was smooth with the tip only slightly smaller than the length of it, though there was a very faint difference to be had there.

"Are you ready for me, darling?"

Honey nodded breathlessly, though she didn't know how to say what she wanted. She took a breath and spread her legs for her husband, thighs tucked up around his hips. The bunny still had to hold on to his shoulders to keep herself up and in place, considering it would have taken a lot more abdominal strength to sit up in that position otherwise, but that was just a small note in their coming together.

It was better, so very much better, to feel his cock pressing inside her, stretching her open as she groaned and rocked her hips forward the little that she could. It was simply right to have her husband's shaft inside her, even after all the years they'd spent together, heart lifting with love for him.

Honey would tell Basil just how much she loved and appreciated him afterwards, of course. There was no better way, however, to spend an evening than with his shaft inside her, her husband sweetly keeping her attention from worrying about what she was baking and the timer imminently going off.

"Mmm, oh… Basil!"

She moaned and clung to him, her bunny ears bouncing as she took his shaft, though she was not in all that much of a position to grind on to him. But his shaft hit all the right spots inside her and one reason bunnies were so prolific in their species was due to just how sensitive their sexual organs were.

So, she didn't need any further stimulation, despite the aching nub of her clit begging attention, to reach orgasm. It came patiently but smoothly, as if it was a path she had walked time after time before.

Her moans tangled with his as Basil gave a bunny-like grunt, which was almost something of a honk, and thrust harder. Every rock of his hips sent him powering into his wife, her succulent folds wetly clinging to his cock as if they were trying to hang on to him for as long as possible. That was not a bad thing, though the moment was swift, despite everything, Honey's heart surging as Basil thrust and thrust.

She groaned, leaning back a little to get a little pressure on just the right spots, though her high came surging for her all the same. The bunny cried out as her husband thrust deep and brought her over the edge, her pussy twitching and pulling around him as she tried to coax his orgasm forth too. He tipped forward as if he was going to push her to the table, though she ached for the moment, revelling in the hot rush of climax as it filled her up.

Basil was not far behind her, the timer going off – but they could leave that just a few moments as he spent himself inside her. As the rabbits pressed together in bliss, he pressed his cock up inside and ground into her pussy with short, sharp strokes, barely even daring to pull back in the slightest as liquid bliss seeped from him. His shaft was bare, but that was not a problem at all to them if they ended up with another kind of bun in the oven too.

He kissed her passionately, their lips melding together perfectly as they enjoyed their afterglows. Ah, the fervour of orgasm was fleeting, but they could seek it again and again, whenever they pleased.

And that was exactly what the bun husband and bun wife would find themselves doing once they'd finished all their baking for the night.

Doing it, as always, as many times as they wanted.

Like bunnies.

Vacation

The red fox sprawled out, eyeing up his partner as she rested on the bed, one leg kicked out before her and the other knee bent. She was beautiful, just like that, Lily stretching out a little more, though the badger was not aware that he was watching her. Kale's red fox brush flicked back and forth, though it was a subtle manner of communication that was rarely paid due attention in those days of anthros. After all, they could communicate far more clearly with words, even if those body language quirks were helpful also, at times.

Kale stood slowly, the fox's shirt off, wearing only a pair of loose shorts in their vacation accommodation. With it being Autumn, he had not thought he'd need shorts but always brought one pair along with him, just in case – which had more than paid off that time. The heating in their cabin seemed to be broken, or perhaps it was just always on the warm side in there. At least they could both be perfectly comfortable when they stripped down a little.

Seeing Lily in her underwear, however… Hey, they might have been together for a few years, but it always got him going. Even when the badger, with her grey fur and striking, elegant stripes in white, was changing in their bedroom back at home, he couldn't take his eyes off her, sneaking looks just so he didn't put Lily on the spot. She surely deserved to be able to change her clothes in peace!

Still…the fox loved her. Her mind, her spirit, her soul, her body. Every part of her. Especially the thick, round curve of her ass, however.

What? He could be crude sometimes too!

"I see you staring, foxie…"

Lily grinned faintly, flicking her eyes up from her book, though she hadn't really been reading it anyway. She always said she was going to read more, but books hadn't been her thing. It was just something that came up in conversation and then she took a book or two away with her on vacation because she felt guilty. There was just something in her head that stopped her visualising things as clearly, which was why, when younger, she'd found herself diving headfirst into comics. They still told a story but in a way that felt more accessible to her personally. Still, she wished there was a way she could get into a good story and lose herself for hours in the way Kale did. He looked pleasantly far away when he was nose deep in a fantasy novel.

Her fox looked up at her with an easy smile, raking his eyes over her body. The badger hadn't worn one of her favourite pairs of lingerie that day, however, to not have him stare at her, perfectly comfortable in it. He hadn't worked out yet that she'd turned the heating up in the cabin, though she didn't mind seeing him barer than he usually was. If only she could get him to lose the shorts too.

However, it didn't look like Lily had to do anything all that much more, not as he eased on to the bed with her, a smirk on his lips. She crossed her legs, tucking the treat of her sex away, if only for a moment. She took a breath as she lowered her book a little.

"Is there something you want?"

The fox nodded, panting lightly, his tongue fluttering between the lines of his teeth.

"Mmm, always you…" He glanced out the window, ears twitching. "And, since it's such a rough day out there, the wind picking up as it is… Maybe I should just stay in with you, keep you company?"

She chuckled, her nose twitching.

"What, no hike for you today, darling? Not even around the lake?"

Yet Lily already knew what was going on and was ready to give him a tease, leaning back against the pillows on the bed where she was propped up. Her bra cupped her breasts perfectly, leaving a dip of cleavage between them, her thicker body curvy and delicious – even if she said so herself. Her wide hips and soft thighs added to her image, everything coming together in a way she was more than comfortable with.

"No… I don't think so…" The fox said, feigning disappointment as he crawled over her and dipped his muzzle lightly. "But I wouldn't want to disturb you from your book either…"

She chuckled, giving up the pretence. They would not head out anywhere that day, not with the lure of the soft bed and sheets under them.

"Mmm, that's okay…" The badger chuckled, tossing her book aside. "Can't say I've ever been all that much into reading anyway… Mmm… Not when you're here to distract me."

With that, the fox tumbled into her arms as he rolled with the badger, so he was on the bottom and she was on top. Just the grind of her body over his crotch and against his front was enough to get his sheath plumping up a little more, revealing his shaft, the tip pushing out more and more. He had always been quick to become aroused, though that was not a bad thing at all, as long as he could last where it mattered to him.

"Mmm… We're going to spend a lot of time here today, aren't we?" Lily murmured as Kale kissed her neck and between the tantalising dip of her breasts, across the rise of her flesh. "I hope… Ah… There's enough food in…"

He chuckled, nuzzling at her and helping the badger sit up a little, so he could unfasten the back of her bra.

"Don't worry, I already pre-ordered dinner for later," he said. "And there's a light lunch for us in the fridge here already."

The cabin may have been small, but it was equipped with everything they might have needed while they were there, although Kale and Lily didn't want for much, not lie that. He licked his lips and kissed her warmly, his paw sliding down her body to seek her underwear, the lacey edge of her panties brushing his fingers.

The fox moaned into the kiss, though Kale knew his partner well and that first round between them was just going to set them up for more fun still that night. He grunted, shuddering a little, though the heat of his erection, fully hard and swollen, was more difficult than ever to ignore.

Lily whimpered into the kiss, a little breathless. Oh, that was not quite something she had expected, in all honesty, though the badger wanted more, shivering against her partner and rocking her hips down against him. His fingers brushed her pussy and she squirmed impatiently, wanting to be out of her lingerie fully even then.

"Mmm, don't make me wait, darling…" She breathed, breaking the kiss. "I want you… Inside me, now."

He blinked, drawing back a little.

"I thought you'd want me between your legs first," he teased, flicking his tongue out as if to highlight exactly what he meant by that. "Lapping and teasing… Orgasm after orgasm…"

"Mmmph, no."

It wasn't quite what she needed, no. The thrill of penetration, coupled with other stimulation, was what she yearned for, after all, even if a little oral play was fun from time to time. It just wasn't her thing personally, preferring his fingers and toys.

He dropped his shorts quickly and she moaned aloud at the mere sight of his cock, her pussy clenching down around nothing. Already, Lily imagined just how he was going to feel inside her, that perfect cock that fit her like no other ever had. Or maybe it was the connection between them that had made things as special as they were, for she had always needed a deeper, more intimate relationship with another before actually getting into sex. Previous partners had fallen short of that, sometimes pressuring her to have that kind of intimacy too before she was ready.

Yet Kale had always taken his time with her and learned her little likes and dislikes – which, in a way, was really the bare minimum. It was more the effort Kale went to with it that made her tingle all over, warming at the notion of him.

She took the lead, however, liking what she liked and wanting what she wanted. Maybe that was an overly simplistic way of putting it, though the badger rolled over on to all fours and thrust her rump back, letting him ogle the thick round of it. Her tail twitched, pushing over the top of her panties, and the fox eagerly dragged off her underwear, though it didn't come all that easily. Her panties snagged on an ankle and he worked them off with difficulty, panting with need, though the badger didn't make it easy for him as she dropped to an elbow.

Showing off her pussy to him, she spread it by reaching back between her legs, two fingers sliding back and forth through her wetness, glistening on her folds, as her arousal grew swiftly. She had to twist a little to get into position and the fox hastened to oblige her, even though he could have taken his time and lapped into her pussy instead, savouring that sight and taste.

It wasn't what worked for them, however, and he moaned, positioning himself on his knees behind her on the bed, the mattress bowing under their combined weight. The bed squeaked and creaked a little, perhaps older than theirs back home, and he twitched one ear at that, though it seemed to be stable enough.

That was enough for the fox as he followed the lines of desire in his body, positioning himself with his cock at her entrance. All it took was a slow, purposeful roll of his hips to push inside her, her pussy stretching lightly to accommodate his meat. He was a moderate size, however, even if he had a fat knot that would swell at the base when he was ready to cum, and there was little resistance to him pushing inside.

"Mmmph…"

It was perfect, however, her pussy squeezing around him, rippling erratically. Or maybe that was his just mind trying to make sense of everything he was feeling, the aching tingle pulsing through his cock. He whined throatily, twisting his head back and forth, though his partner rocking her hips back on to his shaft sent a deep, aching shudder through him.

Ah… Yes, that was better. There was nothing better than feeling his partner's eagerness, the badger's thick body rocking back on to him, her need practically palatable in the air. Even though she was on all fours, facing away from him, the badger was more in control than her fox partner was, thrusting and humping back on to her length.

She knew exactly what she wanted, after all, and let out a heady moan as Kale leaned forward, wrapping his arms around her, just letting her do what she wanted with his body driving into her. It was not passive, though it was close, it was intimate – and it was so perfect exactly the way it was.

"Mmm... Ah... Thank you, love..."

She panted breathlessly, smiling with an open mouth. Lily just had to let her fox know how he was doing everything right for her, how much she appreciated him.

Next time... she'd show him just how much she appreciated him, with her body, too. Things were a give and take between them, of course, neither one dominating everything.

"Mmm... Of course, darling... Mmm... Oh, you feel so good..." Kale groaned, eyes mostly closed, though he leaned into the moment, letting her back rise against him, following the lines of her body. "Ah... You're so wet... already."

"Because I want you."

That was enough for the fox, thrusting a little harder, though he barely drew back at all before grinding back into his partner. Long thrusts were not needed, not when they were not Lily's preference, pushing deep and staying there, as if his knot was already swollen and locking their bodies together.

The bed creaked and the wind picked up orange and gold leaves beyond the window, though that only brought a light smile to his lips. The outside world could wait while he spent all the time he needed with his mate, her wet pussy gripping him as he rolled his hips, rocking in fervent, jabbing thrusts.

The badger moaned under him, slowing her grinds back on to his cock, trusting him more to take her. He straightened up a little more, gripping her hips, though one paw slid around to the front of her crotch to tease her clit. There was more to sex, after all, than merely thrusting, and he wanted to take care of every nuance of her pleasure he could.

For Lily was all that mattered, day and night, forevermore. And that was more than okay with the fox.

"Ah… Kale…"

She moaned his name, heat twisting and curling within her. Yet she quivered in place, her entire body delighting in everything fox gave her, even as Lily passed a little control back to him. It was something they tended to switch roles in, always taking things lightly and lovingly, just to see where things went.

His knot grew and she moaned, loving how it tugged at her pussy. It brought her into the moment, even though it was not large enough, not yet, to lock inside her, pulling in and out of her sex while her entrance was stretched. She arched her back and unconsciously put her body at a better angle for him to grind into her, hitting her G-spot with every stroke. In that instance, it was more of a happy accident that he hit just the right angle, though it was one Kale knew to lean into when all came together so perfectly.

He groaned deep in the back of his throat and she whimpered, licking her lips, trying to stay where she was in the moment, panting heavily. His chest heaved for every breath he dragged into his lungs, though Kale was comfortable where he was, taking short, sharp strokes of his cock, his knot throbbing up thicker still.

To the point that it would not even pull out of her pussy. It swelled deeper inside, her body aching around him, though Lily drifted, panting through an open mouth. She tried to rock back against him, though she needed to take things easy in the moment, everything building to a high like no other.

And it was Kale and only Kale who could bring her there, his fingers trapping her clit and rubbing it, squeezing down – though never applying too much pressure. Even when pleasure was overwhelming him, he always had her pleasure at the forefront of her mind, ripples running through her body as she groaned deeply, something tensing inside her.

That was all she needed, aching for more ecstasy still, her pussy tightening around him, trying to milk him of his seed. The mess of orgasm meant they'd most likely take a shower together afterwards, though the moment was to take for their own right then and there.

So, she languished there, letting it all roll through her, from the shudder of his body up to her backside, the grind of him into her body. His knot was a point of tension, throbbing lust spilling over, though Lily's arousal slickened around his cock, ensuring he could still pump back and forth, snapping above her as he swallowed a curse.

"Ohhhh…"

Lily tried to twist, her hair falling forward a little around her face. She hadn't even thought about that, though it seemed to have come undone from her messy bun as they made love. Yet it was rougher and more carnal as he drove into her, a wave of pleasure rising inside, a wave that she didn't want to stop.

"Mmm… Ohhhhhh!"

And then she groaned long and low, shuddering as he circled her clit, orgasm ripping through her. Yet it all came with a deeper, aching pulse that rang through her, making her judder and rock against him. Yet it was all down to Kale to carry her through that moment, his knot fat and swollen inside her, barely able to take the sudden clench of her pussy around him.

He cried out sharply, a yip that cut through the air, yet the moment was right and it was not for Kale to hold on for a single moment longer. He had to let it all come, to let it play out, as orgasm swelled inside him. It strained, like his knot bristling against the very flesh that held it fast, and he howled as he slammed in crudely, his cock as deep as it could go, his paw falling away from Lily as need demanded everything of him.

And, in that moment, the fox gave Lily everything he could, erupting inside her as spurts of cum shot from him. It was not over productive, but it was all he could give, his hips juddering up to her rump, not able to pull back, but luxuriating there. Their relationship, and sex life, may not quite have fallen in line with conventional means, but it was what worked for them.

And that was only one nuance of pleasure yet to come, leaning over her once more to kiss the back of her neck and nuzzle into his badger. The fox's lips parted in a breathless smile, settling to his orgasm, her pussy wet around him, though nothing leaked out around the tight seal his knot made within her sex.

All was right with their world, easing into the moment and letting it take them. They didn't have to do more that night – yet they would, that first round only a warmup, just for them.

He flicked his tail proudly, pressing his muzzle reverently to her back and taking a deep breath. Yes… Kale was right where he wanted to be, where he needed to be. And nothing else mattered.

With Lily, his holiday was all he needed and so much more.

Quickie

It wasn't the most comfortable of positions to be in, to say the least, though the hare did not mind in the slightest, her heart racing. Her husky partner moaned, at least parked up at the side of the rode while she slid her lips luxuriously over his cock, taking his hard length deep into the back of her throat.

"Oh… Izzy…" He panted heavily, tongue lolling out from his mouth. "Jeez… Where… Why did you even think of this? Ah… Fuck…"

Yet Zack couldn't get all that many words out of his mouth, not with darkness having fallen around them and her lips sealed so very sweetly around his cock. Izzy's grey ears twitched, hints of brown fur struck through the dominant, grey overtones, and he rested his hand between her ears, where her brown hair had been trimmed into a pixie cut. She said long hair felt weird on her, always bristling and tickling around her face, so she usually had it trimmed shorter. Not all anthros had hair like that, as Zack did not, but he liked the look of it on her.

She wouldn't have been his spicy hare if not.

The dog moaned again, shifting his weight from one buttock to the other. Trying to take a breath, it came in shuddery and jumpy again, like his lungs weren't quite working as before, his guts churning and swirling with emotion and need. His knot was not yet swollen, but it did not feel as if that would take long at all as he grunted in the back of his throat, not with the hare's lips around him.

Izzy shivered, her tail twitching, though it was tucked away inside her clothes that time, wearing a short skirt that was only as short as it was due to the sheer length of her legs. She was tall, especially for a hare, and had a lean sense of self with a narrow waist. She didn't spare much of a thought to her physical appearance, though always made sure she was presentable enough for her office job.

Maybe it was the boring nature of her job, however, that had the hare seeking adventure and teases when she was out and about, whenever she wasn't at work. She was more of a thrill seeker than Zack, but the husky was along for the ride – and up for it too – most of the time, which was all she felt she could ask from a partner in that regard. She smiled around him, moaning subtly, enjoying the twitch and pull of his body against her.

There were so many subtle, little notes that came to light when they were forced to be quiet, not all that far off the road, though it was a quiet enough back road. They'd just been coming back from dinner together when she'd unzipped his jeans and fished out his already hardening cock.

Getting him inside her mouth sent a trembling thrill through her like no other, his cock such a vulnerable part of him – yet a part of his body that he trusted implicitly to her. Izzy grunted around him, sliding her lips up and down, mimicking just how it would feel when he was thrusting inside her.

Oh, she wanted that right then and there, grunting deep in the back of her throat, wishing she had both the space and the flexibility to reach between her legs at the same time. Her underwear dug into the soft, plump folds of her sex, spreading her pussy slightly, yet she couldn't get any more sensation than that down there, sucking in a sharp breath through her nostrils.

"Mmmm…"

Izzy pressed on, not sure whether she wanted him to cum in her mouth or find something else, something better; it was hard to consider in the moment, especially when her head was so fuzzy with lust.

"Mmph… Ah… Izzy."

He tried to catch her attention, but the husky could only do so much when he was enjoying everything as deeply as he was. His cock throbbed deliciously within her mouth and the hare even took him into the back of her throat, gulping him down. Even though he was straight, Zack kind of wished he didn't have a gag reflex, just like her. It was really amazing what Izzy could do with his cock, the bob of her ears nothing short of hypnotic as they twitched and flopped. Even though her ears perked, she gave a little twist of her head as she bobbed it, making them sway a little more, though it seemed just like something she did without thinking about it.

Maybe, when the dog's mind was clearer, he'd ask her about it.

"Mmmph… Izzy… Can you…"

Yet the canine couldn't get the words out as he grunted and gasped, swallowing another curse. Not that Izzy was innocent by any means, but he didn't want to spend words like that in her company, not if he could help it, even if Zack could not quite say where that urge came from. The trees swayed above the car, a little cramped, too tight for true comfort, the wind picking up, though the husky paid them little mind even as the hour grew later.

A car swept by, headlights scanning the road, though they paid them no mind. Just the way Zack wanted.

Yet he finally managed to catch Izzy's attention and gently raise her up, though her lips parted breathily from his cock. She panted over him, warm breath tickling his member, and she groaned faintly, casting her eyes up to her husky while the hare swayed her hips, very subtly, back and forth.

"Mmph… Why'd you stop me?"

"I thought you might like something else, hm?" He said, a lazy smile stretching his lips as he recovered himself a little. "Come… Do you think…ah…you can sit in my lap?"

Izzy tried, wriggling over the gear stick and into his lap, though it was hard to spread her legs around him. With her back to the dashboard, there was no doubt as to what she was doing, her skirt hitching up higher still, around her hips and the tops of her thighs, Zack tugging her underwear to the side.

They didn't need more than that to take what they needed from one another. She sank on to him while he positioned his cock for her, the tapered tip sliding deep as she moaned aloud, her head falling slightly back.

"Ah… Yes…"

He moaned too as her wet heat closed around him. She was tight, though never so tight that he couldn't push into her, though Zack had not quite expected to find her as wet as she was that time. It sent a tingling thrill through him, pleased she was as turned on as she was, panting lightly and licking his lips, though he didn't want to pant too heavily in her face. Even if Izzy had not complained about it or anything like that before, the dog didn't want to take the risk.

In that case, it was only polite.

She ground on him, pressing her lips to his and eagerly trapping him in a kiss, though the close confines of the car felt like they were pressing in around them. They were trapped there, pleasantly so, until they had enjoyed their fill of one another, and Izzy kissed him deeply, lie it was the last time she was ever going to come together with him, in that way. It was not so, yet the kiss had that biting edge of desperate need to it, her pussy clenching around him, trying to grind down, even then, on to the rising swell of his knot.

Zack tried to talk through the kiss, though the husky didn't have the heart to slow her or stop her in any way. Maybe it wasn't a good idea for him to knot her at that time, though she was irresistible when she was like that, taking him by a figurative collar and leash and taking him for the ride of his life! Even in that moment, eyes barely open, the hare was spellbinding, hypnotising, and his paws found their place around her waist, tucking into the light curve of it, though she was narrower than him.

Trembling, he succumbed to it, leaning into her, even though his back was firmly pinned to the car seats. He didn't have any agency in thrusting or filling her, not in that moment, though the hare sank deep and rose and fell shortly, keeping his knot inside her as it swelled.

Although it was not something Izzy had admitted before, she loved the sensation of his knot thickening inside her, slowly pushing against her inner walls and demanding that the velvety heat of her cunny moulded to the shape of him. He was going to fatten up at that deepest point, her pussy bulging out with his knot, whether her body was ready for him or not, though the hare's mind was more than accepting of him, urging her body to keep on and up with him.

And when Zack's paw teased around to the front of her crotch, however clumsily his fingers found her clit, she knew she was right where she needed to be, bucking her hips against him.

"Ah… Yes…" She broke the kiss, faintly, though the hare's lips barely moved away in the slightest. "Please… Mmph… You're going to cum in me."

She changed her mind halfway through what she was saying, meeting his eyes as her paws landed on his shoulders. Holding on to her husky partner, she moaned and rode him for all she was worth, though she could barely move, rising and falling shortly and sharply. His swollen knot lusciously locked their bodies together – and they were there until the end, when it finally softened.

Fortunately for her, she didn't want to be anywhere else and, well…he didn't take all that long, after the deed, to deflate. So, she ground into the pressure of his paw, even though Zack couldn't quite get his fingers into a comfortable position against her clit; the pressure was enough and the shift of her body against the husky was more than enough.

So, she let her body do the talking for her, catching his lips in another desperate kiss. He rubbed at her clit, his motions becoming a little more frenzied in the heat of the moment.

For it was not the hare who got off first, not that time, but Zack, the husky grunting into her mouth and finally letting out a muffled howl. Yet the canine could do no more than that as his cock erupted in long, hot spurts of seed, as if his body was trying to send every last drop of it as deeply up into her pussy as possible.

It was not under his control, not even how his cock pulsed within her, throbbing with desire, though Zack caught her cry of desire as tenderly as he could with his lips, kissing her hard, tongues tangling and sweeping up against one another. He leaned her against him, pressing her clit again and changing the motion of his paw to a back-and-forth rub – which was just enough, with the throbbing swell of his knot inside her, to send her hurtling into climax too.

The hare shuddered bodily, though riding out her orgasm against her husky was all she'd wanted, even as another car drove by, the headlights catching them from a second before moving on. If anyone saw, they didn't say anything or pay any attention to them, which was just the way she wanted it. The risk of getting caught and throwing all caution to the wind was one thing, but Izzy didn't really think she wanted to actually get caught. That may well have taken all the fun out of impulsively following the lines of her lust.

"Mmmph…"

She broke the kiss, panting heavily, her husky's lips on her neck. Yet the moment would drag on sweetly, until his knot softened enough for them to part again and get on their way home.

Taking a risk in car sex paid off…though Izzy's mind was already working on other kinky plans, new things they could try. Her husky kissed her neck, a shiver running through her body.

Yet as long as she was with Zack, Izzy had everything she could ever have wanted and more.

Horsin' Around

Essie giggled as Louie dragged her around the back of the stables, the chestnut stallion's lips wobbling with glee as he towed the mouse, who was considerably shorter than him by a foot and a half at least in height. He could have picked her up and carried her, but things were not to be that light and easy, no, not even with her heart pounding, wind whipping her blonde hair back from her rounded ears.

"Mm, Essie …" He rumbled softly, drawing her into his arms where no one could see them, the breeze rustling leaves on the birch trees, which framed the back horse paddocks. "You look so cute like this… You make me just want to sweep you away and spend all day with you."

Her heart fluttered and she leaned against the stallion's chest, her fingers splayed out across his pecs, though there was a definite hint of crisp, fresh sweat about him. She rode at the stables, keeping her horse stabled there, but he worked there as a trainer – a young trainer, it had to be said, though Louie had a way of working and playing with the horses that had her simply spellbound.

That was how she had noticed him, firstly, in an arena with a horse standing opposite him. He had been so still and so quiet, as if even his breath affected the horse he was with. There was no rope between them – no tack at all, no equipment. And that was strange to Essie, even though she had seen things, of course, about that kind of work before. She'd just always used a bridle and saddle, because that was how she was taught.

But Louie had not been trying to ride the horse, no, but to gain their trust. And it was there that the mouse had witnessed the connection between them, how the slightest shift in his posture changed the energy in that little arena, even though there were other things going on at the stables and in the barn at the same time. It was as if the outside world simply didn't matter to the two of them, not there in that moment, the connection drawing them together something that could never be set aside, not that easily. Not even when the threads were still being wound together.

The chestnut stallion had gone on to gently gain the horse's trust, over the coming weeks, and get them comfortable with a saddle and bridle again, though it was a slower process than Essie had expected. She'd delved into conversation with Louie, wanting to know his secrets, how he made it all work with a horse that clearly had some history and trauma behind them.

She'd never expected to fall for him, for the horse to kiss her softly one moonlit night after turning out their horses in the paddock. But it had been right and the mouse would not have wanted things to be any other way, no. For all had come as it was meant to, the threads of fate sweetly weaving them together.

So it was that she ended up behind his arms on a warm afternoon, her nose buried in his chest, mischief in the air.

"Maybe you should do just that to me then?" She breathed, bravely stretching up on to the tips of her toes to kiss his nose, though Louie had to dip his muzzle obligingly even then for Essie to reach. "Sweep me away… Oh, the chores can wait, surely…"

The stallion chuckled, shaking his head, though his brown eyes shone with liquid warmth for her.

"Oh, Essie… You know I'd love that, but the horses still need to be fed and looked after."

She grumbled, even though she knew chores still needed to be done. She might have been able to blow off work for herself sometimes (everyone was guilty of taking a sick day that wasn't really a sick day at times), but it was a lot lower stakes for her in an office job. Louie had actual animals to look after and he took that seriously. She probably wouldn't have fallen for him as hard as she had if he had not cared like he did.

"Mmm, I know," she breathed, brushing his lips with hers. "A little time then… Maybe."

The stallion nickered agreeably against her lips and scooped her up into his arms, his hands cupped under her buttocks while her arms quickly latched on and up around his neck. It was a natural position for them to kiss in, when they were both upright, for the height difference between them proved challenging sometimes, especially with Louie's longer neck and the arch of it. Sometimes, anthros had to get creative when some species, like mice, were on the smaller side. Horses could vary.

She scooped her legs around his waist and he leaned back against the rough wood of the barn, worn from the weather, though it was warm and dry at that time. The stallion kissed her passionately, the soft fold of her lips against his simply where he belonged, sinking into the moment as if he never wanted to come out of it again. Louie could not have said how lucky he had been to have the little mouse walk into his life as if she had been there all along, their relationship swiftly growing and strengthening, but the stallion would never have had it any other way.

He nickered softly into the kiss, his shoulder blades pushed back into the wood, though he couldn't hear anyone else near, not even as his petal-shaped ears twitched back and forth. The sunshine warmed his bare arms and yet not even Louie could miss the heat pooling in his crotch, his sheath tingling with the mouse pressed up so close to him.

Hm…

He tried to control himself, shifting his weight and clenching other muscles, though that was a tall order indeed with the mouse pressed up close to him, her breasts against his chest. Her warmth seeped into him, as if it was something they were sharing, and he could not resist a soft roll of his hips up, following that lure of instinct.

It was just so good to have her in his arms, their tongues dancing softly between their lips. Kissing was not something that had ever been all that much of a challenge to them, though that was because they had always taken it slowly, exploring every little nuance before diving in to more. That was not to say there had not been some sloppier, wetter kisses when they had enjoyed a few drinks beforehand, of course, but that was all to be expected. His soft lips simply had found an easy way to move and press against hers, their heads tilted slightly in opposite directions as the mouse let out a breathy little moan right into his mouth.

"Mmmm…"

Oh, how was he supposed to not react to that? He swore Essie knew exactly what she was doing, even if it was something they really shouldn't have been doing at the stables, his sheath plumping out slowly as his soft, yet hardening, shaft pressed out. It did not rise far, taking it slowly, though it rendered an obvious bulge in his looser work jeans, the stallion's heart racing.

Of course, Essie could not fail to notice the effect she'd had on the stallion and she ground down mischievously against him, rolling her hips and using her leverage on him to her best advantage. Breaking the kiss, Louie gasped, heat rushing to his cheeks in a rippling prickle of tension. His red-brown coat hid most of it, though he swore it still rose from his cheeks, crawling down his neck, a soft grunt leaving him as his need made itself known.

Essie's heart pounded, but the mouse didn't seem at all able to find the desire in her to stop, kissing him again just to get that spark of contact back. She just needed the stallion, every inch of him pressed up to her as if she yearned to devour him. With a moan, she twisted her fingers into his mane, not caring where they were, not even that it was more open and exposed than anywhere they had been so forward with one another before. To hell with all that... In that moment, all the mouse cared about was her partner and the heat of him shuddering against her, all his muscle concealing the softness within.

"Mmm... Ah, Louie..."

Her head spun pleasantly, floating as if she was no longer present or rooted in her own reality, though that was a strange feeling indeed to have. But she had Louie there to hold her and to keep her safe, so Essie never had anything to worry about there. As she leaned on him, he could lean on her too – and that was meant far more than merely physically.

Yet it was the physical her body was concerned with right there and then as she nipped at her lip and pulled back, casting him a wanting look. What she wanted, however, may not have quite lined up with what was sensible in the moment as electricity sparked between them, their connection in tune as his hardness rose against her. She was positioned so she could have slid down on to his shaft, if he had been freed from his clothes, and that was an alluring thought indeed. The mouse whimpered softly as the stallion nuzzled into her neck, inhaling her scent with short, sharp puffs of air, nostrils flaring.

"Mmm... I want you," she breathed. "Here... Louie... The back stables?"

He knew it was a bad idea but, well...it was a quiet day on the yard and, as much as he liked to take his time with Essie and spend as long together as possible, they could be quick too. They would have to be quick, avoiding detection, and he carried her like that with no more than a nicker of agreement, the back stables currently under renovation.

They had, however, been used to store some equipment: an indoor barn with a line of stables facing one another, all open with half-walls and windows. The windows let in a stream of sunshine on one side of the barn, dust motes swirling in the air, but it was the pile of hay bales that had been left in the centre aisle that the equine was the most interested in, for they would have to do for what he had in mind.

"This is so wicked," Essie giggled, light-headed with need as he laid her down on some of the lower bales on her back, her arms going up behind her head. "Are we really going to do this?"

Louie shot her a grin, though she caught the flutter of his eyelashes too, how his ears twitched that little more. He always did that when he was really worked up, but Essie had never told him she knew; she didn't want the hose to stop doing it.

"Mmm… If you want to also," he breathed, as if afraid to break the spell of the moment. "Tell me anytime if you want to stop, okay? We don't have to force anything."

"Oh, but I want to."

Essie had never been so sure of anything in her life, the little mouse's heart hammering in her chest. It was risky and she didn't really want to be caught – oh, but the danger of *being caught* was intoxicating as hell too! Her skin prickled with need and she whimpered as Louie dragged his hand slowly down her chest, between her breasts, her body arching up into his touch as her slim tail curled against the bales.

There was an old but clean horse rug under her head and upper back, somewhat protecting her from the scratchiness of the hay, though the mouse didn't care.

She wanted to be there and she was going to deal with any little discomforts needed, all so she and Louie could get what they wanted.

There was nothing wrong with that. Not as he kissed her neck and toyed with her jodhpurs: tight trousers that stretched over her legs and hugged her figure for riding. They wouldn't come off easily, but the stallion softly slipped off her boots for her, along with her socks, helping her out of the jodhpurs too, for those would have to come off if they were to have their fun.

"Mmm… Louie…"

She breathed out his name as he nuzzled into her inner thighs, not wasting any time as he nestled in close to her, his fingers tracing a path over the muscle of her legs.

She grunted but Louie held Essie fast as he nuzzled down there and the mouse willingly parted her legs for him, all so he could slide his questing lips up against the warmth of her sex. Of course, he had not slipped off her underwear, just so she could cover herself again in a hurry if anything did at all go awry, but that was by the by. He pressed in closer, his thick, fleshy tongue sweeping against the edge of her underwear line, slowly pushing it aside and sliding by.

His mouse grunted and rocked her hips up to him, but he just wanted to make sure she was more than ready for him as he moaned, open-mouthed, warm breath tickling her sex. With the tips of two fingers, so he wouldn't disturb Essie too much, he tugged her underwear to the side enough to expose her plump soft, folds. Oh, he could have spent hours down there, between her legs, pleasing her, sliding his tongue inside and flicking it up against her clit, though he did not delve deep, not yet. He just enjoyed the moment, the light taste of her on his tongue, how her folds parted to his touch, not needing to use much pressure.

And she was wet already, her breath hitching above him. Louie was sure he was getting to her though the stallion was still very much aware of the need for speed, his cock as fully hard and throbbing as it could get in his jeans. Dipping his tongue deeper, he thrust it as deeply into her pussy as he could, lapping up inside her, eyes half-lidded with pleasure Louie would never have concealed.

As long as the horse was with his lover, he was at home. Everything was well with him and he'd never have anything to worry about, no, not in the slightest. He moaned into her sex as the mouse gave a soft squeak, though they were both well-aware of the need to be quiet.

"Ah… Louie… Please…"

He didn't pull away, however, not yet. It didn't feel like he'd spent very much time down there, no, not at all. He wanted to savour her, her arousal marking his lips, though he couldn't lap it off quickly enough, enamoured with her scent. The stallion's tail flagged and swished, a long lash of hairs batting the backs of his legs, though it was not as if Louie could ignore his own need for all that much longer either.

They could be caught…and the horse wasn't at all sure whether he would have preferred to be so revealed with his jeans down and his cock out or not having done the deed at all. He snorted softly at his own folly, though it was not a question he spent much time pondering. Not as the mouse wriggled before him and moaned his name plaintively.

She blinked up at him through a haze of lust as the stallion stood back, fishing out his shaft, the hard, dark-skinned length throbbing into his head. The flat head ached and was even slightly flared already, just enough to give it shape, but he had always had definition there like that. With her partner baring himself, even if only partly, before her, Essie moaned, curling her toes as her tail, even then, tried to tuck itself to the side and out of the way.

The first time they'd had sex, they'd thought his cock would not fit inside her, but, well, they'd just had to take it slow. It was a rather big cock, as was usually the case for equine anthros, but they could work around that without too much trouble, even if the full length would never fully fit inside her. Her body, however, could be persuaded to give up a little more room with him, with a change in angle too from time to time.

So, they enjoyed one another and she spread her legs for him, bending her knees and allowing them to splay out to either side of her body as he moved into position. It looked like the stallion had laid her down on the bales at such a height that she was at a moderately good height for him to push into her and Essie quivered as the head of his shaft pressed to her pussy, encouraging her folds to bow in slightly from that pressure alone.

"Mmm, Essie…"

She moaned as he breathed her name like a kiss, his shaft sliding inside, slowly but surely. It was always a stretch to take him as her body tried to squeeze around, warmth and pleasure seeping deeper and deeper inside her. The head of his shaft popped inside and the mouse could not stop herself from letting out a squeak of pleasure, her tail flicking away, as if she couldn't even control that part of her body. But she didn't have to be in control, not as warming pleasure rolled through her, pulses of need rising increasingly swiftly, her body already primed for the heat of his shaft to burrow as deeply inside her tight sex as it possibly could.

The moment was right as the stallion thrust, grunting over her, and she could just imagine, even in that moment, how his tail was lustfully flagging, swishing back and forth. Yet Essie could not hear all that much besides the rustle of hay under her back, his grunts in her ears, though it was clear Louie was trying to be as quiet as possible. Louie, however, had always been something of a vocal lover (she never kept the windows open in summer *before* they went to sleep anymore).

"Oh… Yes… Ohhhh!"

She wanted to tell him how good he felt inside her, that she wanted more, his cock even deeper, but she clung to him instead, her nose buried into the crook of his neck to inhale his scent. Even then, the stallion was lightly sweaty, his chestnut coat darkening faintly, but it was a clean, crisp kind of sweat that heightened his natural aroma and musk. They could always take a shower later, so it was not as if getting dirty and sweaty mattered to Essie all that much.

His cock just felt too good, stretching her out that perfect amount, though Essie would never have wanted a bigger cock inside her, no. She didn't think she could take anything like that, even when things were as luxuriously intoxicating as they were between them, that perfect combination of love and lust winding together in the best of ways.

The mouse could even feel him throbbing and pulsing inside her, every shudder of his body rolling through her, taking her with long, powerful strokes of his hips. She pressed her paw down over her lower abdomen, once again amazed by how much of his shaft pressed up inside her, the bulge obvious. It did not seem like anywhere near that much of his cock should have fit inside her pussy and yet it did, the grind of that bulge rising through her lower abdomen sending her head spinning.

Essie couldn't get any words out, but the mouse didn't have to when she had her lover there with her, taking care of her. The stallion grunted above her, his tail twitching as he loomed, bearing over her while her legs bent a little more, her knees pointing out a little more so he could penetrate her even more deeply.

"Mmmm… You're amazing, Essie…" He breathed, though the words were barely above a whisper. "I can't believe…unff…I'm lucky enough to be with you."

She whimpered, but he had to keep going, had to give her what she needed. He cupped one hand under her buttocks, pulling the mouse up against him as long, overpowering strokes ground into her pussy, her folds hugging and suckling softly around the girth of his cock. Louie shook his head, nostrils fluttering in a snort, his fingers down at her folds, pressing into her clit just to give his sweetheart a touch more stimulation.

"Mmmph… Not gonna…last too long…"

That was not entirely a bad thing, however, with a limit on their lovemaking. A snorting chuff broke his lips, a bubble of laughter. Was he really doing it with Essie, in the back barn? What if they really got caught? The stakes were high for both of them – and yet Louie still thought, with a dirty part of his mind, that the payoff would all be worth it.

Especially as he rubbed her clit and she bucked up against him, her legs trying to come up more around his waist, though it was as if Essie couldn't get her body to do what she needed it to do in the heat of the moment. But that was okay, Louie giving her clit a light squeeze at the very moment he drove as deeply up inside her as he could, slamming in roughly. It was those combinations of sensations that pushed her over the edge and he knew just how to get her off – even if the stallion had the luxury of eating her out beforehand.

She clapped a paw over her mouth and squealed as orgasm took her, barely even aware of the stretching thrusts of the stallion as he powered into her, giving her every stroke she needed and more. Crying out into the muffling press of her paw, the mouse's body shuddered in wave after wave of climax, pleasure rolling through her, though there was no way for her to control it. Not as Louie ground in harder and harder, her pussy gripping and rippling around him, though there was nothing to hold him back.

Above her, the stallion groaned, nostrils quivering, though she only saw the hazy outline of him as he powered in, stroke after stroke claiming her. And she gave everything she had and was to Louie as he ground in deep and stayed there, trembling, his tail flagged high as his thick flare popped out where it was buried deep inside her pussy.

As his flare bulged, the stallion swallowed his triumphant whinny (damn, that was always a hard one to force down for him) and spent his load inside her. It was such a crude way of putting it but being so wrapped up in one another that they couldn't wait to head home later for their fun was, well…kind of hot too. Pretty hot, in fact, as he kissed her, capturing her lips with his even if he had to bend his neck at an uncomfortable angle to tuck his head down to her. Their tongues flickered out breathlessly against one another, bodies quivering in the pulse of orgasm, though his orgasm, though coming with thick spurts of stallion seed, was briefer and more exultant, at least that time, than hers.

It was over too quickly, but Louie would have sought it out again and again just to be with Essie, to share that moment with her and her alone. The stallion grunted, nose dipping reverently to her as she broke the kiss and caught his nose instead, a hazy giggle on her lips.

They might have taken a big risk in having sex in the barn, but, with the softness of the outside world around them, tucked away from the thick of it, they were right where they needed to be. His arms encircled her, holding her close as he stood awkwardly, holding her tightly, and lay back down on the bales himself with Essie on top of him, her mouse tail slinking softly around his thigh, though it was not as if the stallion was going anywhere.

No… Oh, no. Louie was there with her for good and didn't want to go anywhere else, his cock slowly softening inside her, though they would have to dress again soon enough and get back to where they were supposed to be. Still, it opened the door to more, as their relationship progressed, the two of them remaining experimental, taking things forward bit by bit, more with every day that passed.

Together, they'd always change things up. As long as they were together, nothing else mattered.

Loving Patience

Molly giggled, at the kitchen sink while her partner, Dash, came up behind her. The sheep and the cheetah, well… To say the least of it, they made an odd pair together. Her parents had warned her against getting with a predator species, but things had all worked out better than Molly could have imagined.

"Ah, stop it, you…"

She squirmed against the big cat as he leaned into her, kissing the top of her head and then down the side of her neck, tilting her head softly to the side. Molly quivered, a ripple running through her, although the weight of her wool on her, before the late-Spring shave, made her whole body jostle a little. Molly would be quite glad indeed when she could have that all off! It was a shame her ancestors had grown such thick coats of wool to sell – and, before then, to keep themselves warm through the dreary, wet British winters – as it meant she did the same, but most sheep had learned how to cope with that. Some even still cared for their fleeces and sold them too, which was interesting.

It went without saying, however, that Molly did without wool products for herself. It just always felt a bit icky to her…

"My sweet," Dash rumbled behind her, bearing the nickname from his college years that had stuck, as it was so appropriate. "You work too hard."

His long tail lashed back and forth, the black spots gleaming faintly where the good condition of his coat shone through a little more clearly. Dash purred and nibbled tenderly on her throat, though the wool was not really thin enough there for Molly to feel it as clearly as she otherwise could have.

"Hon…" She said, shivering a little, heat pooling in the base of her abdomen. "I'm not doing any work at all, I'm done for the day."

"Mmm…" The cheetah leaned into her, pressing her waist against the counter in front of her. "Yes, but you're still thinking about work. You think the house needs cleaning, that there's still more that needs to be done… But you don't need to worry about that right now."

"Oh, don't I now?"

She turned around as his fingers curled around her black face, though the bulk of her body, her wool, was an off-white shade. Her cloven hooves matched her face, though she was fortunate enough to have hoof-like, chunky nails rather than actual hooves in place of her hands; she had seen some anthros who bore more of their ancestors than she did. Everyone was special in their own way, however, and there were many accommodations that could be made in the world too, so they had more than enough to get by.

Her cheetah, however, took her breath away each and every time. His brown eyes drew her in and she sucked in a tiny breath, nowhere near enough to satisfy the requirement of her lungs. Molly paused there, spellbound and appreciative of all she had in her life, Dash leaning in closer and closer.

Molly groaned as his lips met hers and Dash rumbled a chuckling purr, parting his lips to draw her in even closer to him, to invite a deeper sort of kiss. He thanked any listening gods every single day that he was fortunate enough to have a sheep as wonderful as Molly in his life, so warm and sweet, always there for him – and keeping him on his toes too. Even though he'd thought she had a quieter personality and was quite contemplative when he'd first met her, four years prior, she had a spark to her and a feisty side. Whereas she was more amenable to finding workarounds for herself in tricky situations, his sweet sheep stood up for others with a vivacious tenacity that hooked him.

"Mmm…"

Dash hummed lightly into the kiss as his tongue swept playfully up against hers, twisting and curling. They had very different muzzles, with his being a little flatter and shorter than hers, though he still had more than enough stretch to part his jaws wide. She didn't need to open her mouth very widely at all, being a herbivorous, traditionally grazing species, so he made sure to accommodate her, even as his tail lashed back and forth.

Oh, you know not the effect you have on me, darling…

He would have said that aloud if he was not pressing in closer, his paws sliding down to the small of her back as he encouraged her body to bow against him. She moulded to the shape of his body as he held her tightly, the sheep's fingers stroking behind his ears, scratching in that special spot that made him quiver.

She knows exactly what she's doing.

Molly grunted, her T-shirt riding up as his paws teased it higher and exposed a sliver of soft belly. There was little definition to her, no hourglass figure that may have been plastered over Cassandra's Seduction, a lingerie company, glossy ads, yet she was everything he wanted. She was strong in herself, more powerful than he had ever expected from a sheep and surprised him in so very many ways.

"Mmm…" She broke the kiss softly, wetly, a string of saliva connecting them for a breath of a moment, though their deeper connection, as ever, remained. "What are you doing to me, love?"

She traced a finger under his jaw and he grunted, blushing a little, though it didn't show through his yellow fur.

"Mmm, just showing how much I appreciate you," he said, drawing her closer, backwards, step by step. "Won't you take a break with me, hon? You have been working very hard, I know. I want to make sure you are taking time for yourself…and getting the pleasure you deserve, of course."

"Oh, is that so?"

Yet it was easy for her, so very easy, for her to let him draw her up the stairs, though Dash couldn't walk backwards the whole way, no. That might have been a little risky, considering he was just trying to get to their bedroom. Even if they'd lived together for a year and a half so far, it still gave the cheetah a little thrill to think of it, and the house they rented, as *theirs*.

There was nobody else he wanted to be with for the rest of his life.

"Molly… Forget everything," he breathed, a smile quirking and tugging at his lips as he took her to the bedroom with him, holding her paws as he walked backwards once more. "You don't have anything to busy your mind with right now, nothing at all. Just come with me… Let me make you feel good."

Molly shivered, his paws sliding over her shoulders, already working on her shirt, drawing it up and over her head. She obligingly raised her arms for him, though sometimes it was a strange feeling to be undressed, taking her breath away to be treated so softly and kindly, as if she was a breakable thing.

Slowly but surely, he revealed every inch of her, down to her lingerie, though he set her clothes aside and folded them (not neatly) on the chest at the foot of the bed. Her eyes followed the hypnotic sway of his tail and Molly cocked her head playfully at him, batting her long eyelashes just to see his step stutter a little, throwing the cat off his game.

"If you wanted to go to bed with me, darling," she breathed, "all you had to do was ask. No more than that…"

"Ah, but they I wouldn't have got to put on the show I did, hm?"

Dash grinned and shrugged out of his shirt, making a lot less of a spectacle of it than he had undressing Molly, even if he ached already to get her all the way down to her wool. He pressed between her legs as she sat on the edge of the bed, readily parting her legs for him, though she trapped him there too, her thighs more heavily wooled than her lower legs.

"Mm, you always put on a show, dear," she said, though still retained some control over the situation, her fingers sliding over his shoulder and tenderly around to the back of his neck. "And I love seeing it every time."

The pressure of her fingers curling lightly around the back of his neck bid him in against her again, kissing her deeply, though the kiss took a lustful, hotter edge that time. It was as if there was a rising throb of need there, as if their arousal had no bounds – but only when they were with one another.

She squeezed her thighs around him, his jeans grinding forward with a larger rise at the crotch than before. Oh, he was horny, she knew he was, and she ached already to have him inside her. Yet her cheetah laid her back on the bed gently, even as they kissed, and he panted hotly, breaking the kiss to slide down her body.

"Let me take care of you first."

Molly squirmed as he shifted out of his jeans, pushing them down and getting rid of his underwear too, as there was really no reason for it to stay there. It was just digging into his rising shaft, smooth with a defined head. In that sense, it was just as well he had not kept the sharply spiked barbs of his ancestors, for that would have greatly reduced how he could please his partners with his cock, even if more sexual pleasure could be enjoyed through other means.

No... Dash preferred how he was, his cock throbbing lightly as it pumped up with blood and he nuzzled down her body, kissing her clavicle and working his way lower, between her breasts, though the cheetah left her bra on for the moment. The sheep panted lightly, her chest rolling with every breath, but he hooked his fingers neatly into her underwear, framing her hips and pussy sweetly, gently sliding them down.

He took his time easing off her underwear, exposing her to his eyes as he panted hotly and the flavour of her arousal danced in the air. Oh, how he needed to be closer to her, so very much closer, his tongue flicking within his muzzle as he contained the sudden drool of saliva within his mouth. One of Dash's favourite places to be was between her legs, eating out her pussy to make her moan so loudly for him.

And that was exactly what the cheetah intended to do as he eased off her underwear down her legs, admiring the curves of her, how he could dig his fingers into her wool and tease her body beneath, though it took more finesse. Not that Dash minded that in the slightest, of course, grunting in the back of his throat, unable to even control the lash of his tail back and forth.

"Mmmm... Lift your legs a little for me, darling."

Molly knew exactly what he wanted of her, sliding her legs up and over her shoulders, though she didn't squeeze to trap the cheetah's head between them, not that time. Dash, however, spared a moment to rub his cheek against her wool, a throaty purr escaping him, his tail flipping up a little as his sheath tightened around the base of his cock, fully swollen.

Ah, he could have thrust inside her, though he longed for more, to take his time with her, kissing the inside of her thighs as he nuzzled down to the exposed folds of her pussy. His lightly skilful tongue swept out against her petals, easily parting them to get at the sweet treat of her heat within. She was already slick around her inner folds, close in to the dark entrance to her sweetness, and he lapped up her arousal eagerly, his flexible tongue digging and curling against her.

She groaned as he pleased her, so easily finding all of her sweet spots, all the little things she liked. Molly's heart skipped a beat and she tightened the grip of her legs against him, without even thinking about it, her mind wandering a little, though the sheep tried to keep her eyes open. She wanted to keep Dash in her sights at all times, though her dark eyelashes wanted to fall over her eyes, warm breath wisping over her lips and from her flared nostrils.

Her moans, however, were all the music he needed as he eased a paw between his muzzle and her pussy, fingers helping to spread her folds briefly, though there was one thing the sheep always loved when he was preparing her body. Slow and steady always worked best for Molly, of course, and he took the time to get her nice and wet for him, her body softening and yielding to his touch as he toyed with one finger sliding gently inside her. The sheep whimpered and he pressed on, working it back and forth lightly, testing out just how wet she was, how deep he could go. For one thing that got her off quickly, and helped her pussy to stretch a little more, was penetration, regardless of how they played it out.

"Mmm… Oh… That…" Molly squirmed, settling herself a little more comfortably on the edge of the bed. "So good… Ah… Dash… You're too good to me, really…"

"Mmm… Only as good as you deserve."

And she deserved all the very best, in his eyes and those of others too – for Dash would never hear anything otherwise, oh no. He knew how much he adored his partner, licking his lips and swiping it up around the nub of her clit as it gently grew increasingly sensitive with blood. He adored when it thickened up a little, growing plumper and protruding more from the small hood of skin that protected it most of the time. Hers took a little more time to push out, though it was just a part of how her body was made up, right at the entrance to her sex.

Once it was obvious, he wrapped his tongue around it briefly in a lewd slurp, hungrily sucking her clit between his lips to suckle on it. The sheep bucked and groaned against him, though he took his cues from the subtle twitches and shifts of her body, working her up slowly.

Throughout it, his cock ached furiously, as if it was being drawn by another kind of need, although he couldn't let himself slip down into that not yet, no. He had to take care of her, to show his sheep how much he loved her, lapping around her clit again and giving her a flicking swipe over it once more. Adding a second finger to her pussy had her arching her back and quivering, thrusting up with all the leverage Molly possibly had on him and the bed.

"Mmmm… Ah! Oh, Dash… Dash, I think…"

Molly wasn't sure she wanted to get off yet, not until Dash was inside her, though it didn't seem, that time, as if she had all that much choice in the matter. His attention was so rapt, so intent on her, that she couldn't help herself, greedily taking everything he offered her and then some.

He grunted softly and shook his head a little, twisting it moderately back and forth to help prevent any aches or kinks in his neck. Dash would have gone through it all, of course, to give her pleasure, pressing deeper, working his fingers back and forth within her increasingly wet, slick pussy. Her sex clung to his fingers with every mimicked thrust, lewdly slurping around his fingers as if even her sex was trying to keep him inside.

Oh, she was ready, definitely ready, but he could give her more than one climax, and Dash caught her clit once more between his lips, flicking his tongue rapidly against it. It was something she couldn't take early on, only when she was close, and he bet he could get her there with it. Grinding his fingers furiously within her, as if he was really over her, fucking her, in that moment, he hissed against her sex, feline need partly getting the better of him.

Yet it was all worth it as she moaned and cried out, a strangled gasp breaking her lips as she shuddered up to him. He tried to get his tongue, briefly, into her pussy as well as his fingers, though the feline would have to wait to taste her sweetness, his heart leaping in his chest. The moment of her orgasm was all he yearned for, time after time again, though his own need ached and throbbed faintly. It was not enough, even then, for it to draw Dash's attention, however, groaning against her to allow even those subtle vibrations to travel into her pussy simultaneously.

She rode out her orgasm against him, moaning in the back of her throat, though she was not too loud, not even in the height of climax. Molly clung to him, her fingers around his head, though he didn't have long hair there, not like some anthros – just his natural fur. His fur poked out between her fingers as she brushed his ear, taking a shuddering, gasping breath, as if she couldn't get enough air into her lungs.

Orgasm claimed her and, giving herself over to it, she breathed more easily, riding out the undulating waves of pleasure, heat tingling through her, giving her so much more than she could have gained on her own. There was just something special about her partner that always meant she climaxed much harder when she was with him, rather than without. Molly just didn't get the same out of masturbating as she did from her loving cheetah.

"Mmmm…"

She panted as she came down, though the sheep was already reaching for him. Clasping his paw in hers, her heart surged, feeling him already rising to meet her.

"Yes… Please…" Molly grunted, licking her lips, heat in her cheeks and tingling down her neck. "I need you… Close to me, inside me."

"Yes… I'm coming, sweetheart, I promise…"

Dash moved fluidly over her, not even taking his own shaft in hand. He knew the curves of her body by that time and she wrapped her legs around his waist, however loosely, the moment she could. He had to bend his knees a little to get to the right height to slide into her, but that was really a small price to pay to push into her, to feel the heat of their bodies coming together in far more than mere carnal lust.

It was about the intimacy for both of them, more than anything else, breath hitching and catching, need rising. She may just have climaxed, but Molly could go again much more swiftly than the cat, so Dash was more than ready to see what more he could coax from her. He mrowled faintly as he bowed over her body as if in praise, though he would always worship her. Maybe that was pushing things just a little too far, but it was something of the dynamic between them, adoration that carried them forward, day after day.

They wouldn't have wanted it any other way. Not as Dash pumped his hips deeply and slowly, sliding the full length of his cock into her wet, slippery sex with every thrust. Her arousal clung to his shaft, overruling even the hint of pre-cum at the tip of his length, though neither minded that. There was more than enough delectable friction as she gripped his cock, tensing around him, the tightness around his cock making the feline want to plunge deeper and deeper.

It was the lure of the sheep, everything that drew him to her, over and over again. Dash kissed her neck, driving deep, every thrust of his hips spearing his shaft into her, her body wrapped around him in the best of ways. He thrust more powerfully, sucking in a breath and a half-muffled yowl, grinding in a little more roughly, following the cues of her body while her legs tightened more sharply around him.

She didn't want him to pull back, not at all, not even as he thrust, driving into her with a rhythm that suited them both. There was no barrier between them, delighting in the euphoria of skin-on-skin contact, groaning long and low, the sound rumbling up from the back of his throat.

"Mmmmm… Mine…"

He growled passionately as he thrust a little harder, his sheep bucking up against him. She was so soft, all over, yet hid a sense of steel inside that could not be truly overcome, no. Molly was her own sheep and she let those around her know that well and truly, even if sometimes it did not come out as clearly as Dash may have liked it.

Some sides of her, however, were just for her cheetah to know and see. Molly whimpered, her throat feeling tight, though she clung to him, her paws on his back, digging into his shoulder blades as she shifted and rolled her hips along with each and every one of his thrusts.

"More… Please…" She gasped out. "Inside me…"

Dash seemed only too eager to please her, thrusting harder and startling another coarse cry from her lips.

"Oh!"

Yes, that was exactly what she wanted, soaring within the sweet trap of his arms as her pussy squeezed sharply around him. It was so hot, his body covering hers, though her wool didn't help much in that regard. Molly moaned aloud and arched her back, grinding down on his cock without thinking actively about what she was doing, though it was all about instinct and the needs of her body in that moment.

Nothing else mattered, no, just being close to Dash, the cheetah leaning over her, lips on her throat, hot, rasping breaths tickling her exposed, vulnerable neck. It then that she climaxed, pushing her hips up, shuddering against him as she once again entrusted her orgasm to him, waves of rocking pleasure swamping her. He powered deeper, thrusting harder, hips coming up flush against her body with every stroke of his cock.

Dash took control of the moment and the movement, grinding into her, though he exulted in her climax even more than he would his own. His eyelids fluttered, on the edge of losing himself, though he held on for a few more moments as he thrust deep, short, sharp thrusts thrusting into her tense, clutching pussy.

It was with his partner's orgasm still rolling on that the cheetah finally got off, yowling throatily as he lost control. He slammed deep and stayed there, quivering, ropes of thick cum spurting from him, filling her pussy. Some bubbled and forced its way back down the length of his cock – probably the angle of their bodies coming together – but it was not their focus, not as Molly swept her paws down his back to where the light hollow was at the base of it.

"Mmmm… You're mine too… Ah… Darling…"

She grunted out the words, nuzzling into him, though settled there, letting his body move against hers, passion simmering. There would be more rounds for them, together, that night, for Dash was not going to let her mind wander back to worrying in a hurry, but Molly didn't mind that. There wasn't really anything for her to worry about, of course, and she liked the world the feline took her to, time after time again, her lungs easing, something she couldn't put a name to unknotting in her chest.

"Mmmm…"

He hummed against her, trapping her lips in a passionate kiss and staying there. She was all he needed, everything, day after day, night after night.

And never would the sheep or the cheetah find themselves without one another.

A Rare Breed

It was not usual for a dragoness to mate with a gryphon drake, but it was right, at least for them, at least for June and Gion, the gryphoness with soft, blue eyes and brown feathers tipped with white, and her partner, the larger, more dominant, red drake with a fierce spark to the set of his head. They would be cast out of their respective tribes if they were ever found out, yet the moment was right with the wind picking up outside their shared cavern, deep in the mountains away from both of their flights of gryphons and dragons, the first spots of rain picking at the air.

"I love you so much…"

Gion purred, the red drake not all that big, but about the size of a draft horse. Dragons grew throughout their lifetimes and, being thirty-two years old, Gion still had many, many years left to grow. He nuzzled between the ear-tufts of his gryphon partner, June, the gryphoness chirping and trilling faintly, her tail sweeping back and forth. If there had not been soft, tawny feathers, speckled with darker shades and white, on her cheeks, meeting her wickedly hooked, yellow beak, she wouldn't have been able to hide her blush as well as she did. It flowed through her, prickling and tickling at her skin, the rain picking up outside, the mountainside green in the flush of summer outside.

It was the perfect time to mate and she knew that to be so as she tilted her head to the side, locking her beak with her dragon's lips, though it was something that she had to think about doing less than she did when they had first courted. Lips did not go as naturally with a beak as she might have liked, but June was where she needed to be, with her lover, lying back on her back with her wings softly folded under her, everything coming sweetly together. As quadrupeds, they matched up well in the line of their bodies against one another, despite the rivalry between their species.

It wasn't as if it was easy to kiss beak on beak anyway… She'd learned and, of course, he was better at it than her. The drake was at least half her size larger than her again, June shivering in his warm, dominating grasp as he cradled her. His wings spread above her as the rain added much-needed moisture to the ground, his crimson tail swinging back and forth lightly, as if it was mimicking her feline-like one, though June was inherently and intrinsically a gryphon: she always would be. Some traits, however, crept through and could not be mixed up with anything else.

She grunted, shivering as Gion kissed down her neck, nipping and nibbling, his sharp teeth offering a myriad of different sensations. The gryphon squirmed under him, her forepaws tucked up to her chest, but her blue eyes shone only with love and trust for him, knowing that there was no way that Gion would ever harm her or treat her badly. One way or another, whatever happened, they were there to stay.

"I love you, darling…" He murmured, kissing her beak gently as June squirmed and chirped. "I'll… We'll only do it if you want to… I promise."

That the dragon wanted her and her body, of course, was by the by, considering the slit hiding his shaft had already parted, allowing a tip of pink to protrude out. It swelled with every beat of his heart for her, his testes held internally, but the fine form of the gryphoness did not appeal to him as much as her mind. Her quick wit, how she could outstrip him in flight, her zest and vitality for life… It was all something that he needed in his life, someone with him until the very end of his days, heart beating harder and harder for her, seeing only June, seeing only the gryphon.

"I want you too," she murmured, though June's eyes could not help but drop to his cock, churring curiously. "Oh… Oh, you're so big…"

Gion shivered, nuzzling her soothingly.

"I will be so gentle with you, only as much as you want, I promise."

But their bodies craved more, June shivering submissively. The gryphoness was led instinctively by, well, true instinct, for it was not as if she had had sex before. That was a crude way to put it, but mating to make eggs did not seem right either, not what she wanted it to be. Lovemaking? Yes… Yes, that fit better, allowed her to ease better into the motion of letting her legs slip apart while she laid on her back, exposing her plump slit to him.

Her body, of course, had to react to everything, the arousal coursing, tickling and tingling, through her body. Never had it been as wet as it was right then and there before, the dragon nuzzling her chest, preening her feathers carefully, all the way down to her fur, where feathers became her tawny, rich hide. Her tail swept back and forth across the cave floor, though the only restlessness she felt was in wanting his shaft.

But the dragon didn't allow her to have it! If her beak could have pouted, she would have done so, but June could only squeak and reach for Gion as the drake's nose quested down her belly, closer and closer to her slit. Yet his cock was easing out increasingly, further away from her, a thick, throbbing length ridged with nodules, thicker towards the base than they were closer to the head. Her body screamed for it, but the dragon had something else entirely in mind.

"Ohhh…"

The first she knew of Gion's secret plan was the swipe of his hot, wet tongue against her pussy, slipping into her slit and through her wetness. She could not help but squirm, prey to her own emotions, losing herself, right where she needed to be as the storm picked up outside, a roll of thunder pealing in the distance, the drake's nose pressing between her legs, under her tail, tongue delving hungrily into her honeypot.

He smirked against her sex as he ate her out, though it was a first time for him. Gion could never feel bad about waiting for so long to have his first time, for having it with June was the best and the only way that he could have imagined losing his virginity. So much was attributed to it, but he had not wanted a dragon mate from the very moment that he had laid eyes on her. It was all that he wanted, all that he craved, the sweetness of her dancing tartly on his tongue, curling it around his mouth just to get up every drop of her taste.

The gryphoness was his heart and soul and he leaned into her, a forepaw on her leg, coaxing it apart a little more so that he could get in a little closer, wanting her, yearning for her, whimpering throatily. He could be vulnerable too, even if Gion was the one who more naturally took the lead, heart leaping and turning over even as his cock throbbed between his legs, hanging there, wanting, waiting.

He didn't know for how long he would be able to hold back, or whether there was any sense in holding back at all, what with his heart pounding for his sweetheart as it was. Every part of his being told him to mount her, to breed her, though Gion knew what would come of their copulation. After that, when the clutch was laid and the eggs, finally, hatched, the hybrid joining of their lives would never again be hidden, and yet he yearned for it, the opening up of their relationship to all eyes.

He would protect her, defend her, give everything for her. But all Gion needed to do in that moment was to slip deeper into her, his tongue curling up inside, tasting her, the velvety wetness of the gryphon wrapped around his tongue. He wanted even more, however, his cock throbbing harder than he had ever thought possible, drooling and dripping – though only lightly when it came to the pre-cum. That was part of his body that Gion, after all, would come to learn more of later on.

"Mmph…" His darling gryphoness, as the storm raged and grew closer outside, squirmed, trying to reach for him, helpless and beautiful, yet safe under him. "Please… Gion… We can… Mmm… I want…you… Only you…"

In a rare fit of control, she squirmed and rotated over onto all fours, standing under him, presenting herself for him in the traditional mating position, where her wings would not be crushed, her hind legs braced for his attention. Her slit dripped with her arousal and his saliva, body ready, mind begging for him – that was if the stream of croons and chirps and moans flowing from her beak were to be believed. Through it all, he caught her verbal pleas, whimpering for him, the dragon moving instinctively, sweetly, over her back, his shaft pressing in eagerly against her backside.

"Are you ready?" He breathed, following her lead, though it was only right in the mating order of things for him to be on top, his wings spread protectively. "My love… Oh, I adore you so much."

And the rock forward of his hips came as soon as she whispered her assent, in that moment their bodies becoming one.

In a rare breeding, he covered her, cock pushing sweetly into her, claiming her body as his for the first time as they could never again take back the moment. He filled her smoothly, only taking her as far as her body could go at a time, gently stretching and spreading out her folds increasingly, taking his time. There was no rush, not really, even with the storm keeping them gently trapped within the cave, though the dragon would have had the moment go on forever, if he'd had any say in the matter. It simply felt too good to feel her heat closing in around him for the very first time, rippling and pulling, though the gryphoness did not have any control over her body, not in that way. It was all instinct, all mating pleasure, everything bringing them together in the most beautiful of ways.

He thrust, filling her, the gryphoness stretching around him, though she was too lost in the moment to cling onto her lover, at least too much. His shaft penetrated her deeply, yet June could not be lost in the mechanics of it at all as her legs buckled and threatened to drop her to the ground, even if her lover was mostly supporting his own weight. The gryphon moaned, head hanging, not knowing before that sex could feel *that good*, to be so close to him, held so tight and so dear, his wings protectively spread.

Her body responded, closing around him, rippling, though she was not in control, muscles contracting that she had not been able to use before. Maybe, in time, June would find herself able to better control her body in more ways, but that would come with practice and experience. In that moment, she was there for her lover mating with her for the first time for lust and love, their first clutch of eggs surely well on the way already, for there was no going back for either of them.

They wouldn't have wanted it to be like that, after all. They wanted each other, only each other. He thrust and thrust, powering into her, his strokes becoming stronger as she crooned for them, toppling over the edge into her very first orgasm. Lust flowed through her, legs trembling, and, still, the gryphon hen held herself up with all the strength she felt she had left in her body, wanting to be there for her partner, to support him through all that she possibly could.

There would be many more mating nights to come as her body hummed with lust, his breath coming more quickly as he pushed deep, aching for release. But that time was their first, a time just for them, a time that would change the course of their lives. For Gion could not hold back as her passage flexed and pulled around him, massaging the full length of his breeding spire, coaxing him to the edge of no return, wings flaring out sharply.

Yet his sweet gryphoness was there to support him, to take the weight of him as he half collapsed over her back in climax, screeching out and dipping his head nearer hers, the gryphon and the dragon, together forever. Ropes of thick, creamy seed flowed deep, designed to be sticky and clinging for the act of mating in flight, but she trembled powerfully under him, holding fast, wanting it all.

"I love you," June breathed. "And I never want to be without you."

It was the strongest conviction he had ever heard from her, heart lifting, soaring, more so than it did while he was touching the clouds with his wing tips in flight. For Gion knew, at once, that there would never again be any other in his life and the world, his seed flowing deep, hastening to quicken the eggs ready and waiting inside her.

With their family to raise, their lives were forever bound, forever together, exactly as the rare breed of gryphon hen and dragon drake wanted.

As his shaft throbbed within her, spending the last, thick drops, the hen's pussy contracted around him. She was already ready for another round.

And a gryphoness in heat, now that she'd had her first time, was not to be denied…

A Conflict in Classes

Kasha giggled, the quadrupedal, golden dragon spinning and twirling in the forelegs of her suitor. He was taller than her with scales of royal blue and the horns on his head curled up at the ends like those of the traditional devil, although if he was anything of a devil, he was simply devilishly good-looking. His good looks had been what had caught her eye but even Kasha knew that there was nothing of substance behind those eyes, the light of a smile never reaching them as he spun her in her shimmering sky-blue ball gown, the dragoness wanting to know him, wanting to love him but, well… Everyone knew that there wasn't anything there.

She was twenty-one and almost too old to be married off in a modern culture that knew wealth and riches, the majority of the dragon-world automated in magic. Sure, the feral creatures could fly, spreading their wings, but they still walked on all four legs most of the time, holding true to timelessly old customs and times that had well and truly made them who they were.

Dragons would thrive but the families in power, nobles and the like, still traded the treasure of their young dragonesses between one another, gathering pleasure and influence wherever they went. It was archaic to expect their females to marry into other families and yet it was a practice that continued with them being groomed for it from a young age, shown that they had no other option or path in life to take regardless of what they may well have wanted for themselves otherwise. Not all, of course, fell for it, but the troublemakers were few and far between.

Yet Kasha's smile was fixed and he did not see. Her forelegs snaked around his neck, seeming to draw him close, and that was still a lie. She knew the game and she played it well as her grand suitor from the family of Davenport, who coincidentally preferred to go by his last name and family name, held her in the eyes of all, dancing across the grand ballroom of a mansion that really was too large for her family. There was no reason for her to leave, of course, forsaking her studies, but her family tremored with greed for more power and wealth, extravagances beyond their wildest dreams. And everyone wanted to sink their claws and teeth into a gold dragoness... Truly, she had been an easy sell.

"Davenport..." She breathed, eyes alight as she played the game. "You take my breath away!"

The drake smirked and winked, tongue flickering out, a dimple showing at the corner of his lips as if he could not help but let it show.

"My dear... Our wedding shall be beautiful, the talk of the country. I cannot wait to see what you plan."

Her smile wavered and yet she disengaged with a giggle, feigning that she needed to adjust her dress, tail sweeping back and forth, the rustle of cloth softening even in such a musically gentle environment. The orchestra played on and she curtsied prettily as he bowed in turn, ever one to follow right along with social formalities at all times. He needed to, of course, put on a show for her too for it was all a tactical manoeuvre on the part of his family but Davenport was only so good of an actor, which was not all that good.

"Excuse me," she murmured demurely, sinking lightly back into herself. "I must retreat to the powder room. Will you wait for me?"

His answer came but she was not listening, trading smiles and pleasantries as she made good her swift exit. The dragon left a foul taste in the back of her mouth, but her heart pounded, one more thing that she needed to do throbbing through her, a pulsing, pounding drive that would not release her. She was promised to Davenport to be married, of course, but there was one other who had always been in the wings, hoping for her, waiting for her, yet ultimately never to be with her.

And, still, she'd promised him time for one last goodbye.

She burst into her private quarters – a section set off from the ballroom just for her to dress and pretty herself in close proximity to events – in a bustle of dress, lips pressed together and her facade dropped. And yet no one could ever have said that Kasha was not beautiful as she hastened past lines of mirrors, lit with the magic of dragon-fire, her reflection glistening and gorgeous and entirely not in need of the powder room in the slightest.

Where was he? Her heart leapt into her mouth and she gulped, eyes wide even with the make-up that accentuated the finer, lighter scales there. Did Carson not want to see her? Was it really all going to be over, her wedded bliss rapidly approaching, without even so much as a goodbye?

Kasha swung her head from one side to the other, although there were few hiding places in her quarters, a curtain shielding and softening the far side of the room even as she rushed for it. Was that his scent on the air? The outdoors… The earthen musk of a hunter?

"Carson… Carson, are you here?"

And then his body was against hers, the sensation of the larger drake overwhelming her before she had even caught his name or whisper on the still, cloying air of the ladies' quarters. Their lips collided and they moaned into one another's mouths, tipping their heads to the sides so that their jaws could lock, tongues tangling in desperate, heady lust. Kasha could not even care that her make-up was smudging, her mane dishevelled in how it lay down the long, sensual arc of her neck, as long as she had him pressed heatedly to her, where he needed to be.

"Carson..."

He nuzzled her cheek, stealing kisses from her, the grey dragon's eyes soft and yet intense, both at the same time. Kasha trembled up to him, moaning for the taste of him again, and yet she yearned too to take in the sweep of him, those lovely, curved horns and the frill rising back from his cheeks. Those brown eyes would be what called her to him over and over again, heart pounding, desperate for him, those spotted scales so intimate in their detail even if they did not have the shine of royalty.

Kasha whimpered, shuddering. That was because his heart shone instead, his personality lending the true light to him that those who surrounded her in the daily act of her life simply did not have. A hunter, he travelled and only came to her home in the mansion on occasion, although those times were fewer and farther between as her parents suggested that she would be better off socialising with dragons that, well, she may be suited to marry one day. And they would never, not even once, accept Carson to take her claw in a date, let alone the rest of her life.

The thought of him leaving clawed at her soul and she couldn't breathe, eyes wide and straining, tail shaking, the shiver running through her body, setting her scales on edge. Why did it feel so right to have him pressed up against her, her body luxuriously conforming to the shape of him as if they had always been meant to be with one another, secured and wrapped up in a tail and scales that they both knew so very intimately.

"I need you," she whispered, lips on his throat, pressing down. "Oh, Carson, I can't do this, I can't go through with it!"

And then he was on her, a savagely enthusiastic growl tearing itself from his lips as if that was just what he'd been waiting to hear, words coming out in a whispered hiss of a growl. His eyes – oh, those were closed, she didn't need to see them, only needed to feel him as he pinned her sensually, the lounging sofa in the corner of the room providing at least a soft rest for her head. Her body, however, bore down to the floor, the thick carpet bowing to the unyielding of her scales, pinned and held there – willingly so.

It was right to be there, but Carson's claws tore through her clothes with deadly intent, an intent that did not seek to take something from her but to deliver it back to her tenfold. He moaned, breath hot and harsh against her neck, Kasha whimpering, lips moving without any words coming out.

For there was something hot and hard driving against her stomach as he pushed over her, hind legs scrambling, but neither of them had the will to stop what had so very clearly begun without either calling it to the forefront of their attention. No dragoness could fail to know what that was – she'd had to speak to the other dragonesses in her family about the ways of mating for they, at least, wanted to prepare herself for her wedding night. A virgin by choice until she found the right one to take her virginity, the precious flower that she held dear, her mother had not seen fit to give her the talk, even if she had found methods elsewhere to build her understanding.

And now his cock pressed against her, the shaft that could promise so much pleasure, mating joys, Kasha's eyes wide and lips parted, yet unable to do anything to stop it.

Oh, she needed it and she wanted it. She hadn't had a drop of wine that night and everything she did was well and truly her choice, she knew that. She just hadn't expected it to come in a rush, a moment that had to snatch for herself as Carson murmured her name lovingly over and over again, a fearful tremble in his naked scales, body bare of the garb of royalty, those who perhaps thought that they were better in the world than they were. He could be as he was and she needed that, that seductiveness that was genuine and real, the sweetness that he wasn't putting on.

And yet...

"We may not..." She whispered, although her moan as his lips trailed a path down to the trembling rise of her proudly curved chest told a different tale. "Oh... Carson..."

But Carson knew that he had her and he could only have her at once before she was married off to a dragon who didn't even know who she was. Her favourite colour, performance, background, history, younger years... None of that even mattered to them as long as her pussy was there to do its job! He was the only one that knew her and he tore her dress off entirely, growling as he kissed her,

"No..." He hissed, eyes narrowed in dark intent, the fuel to his fire that made her howl with need, twisting and contorting beneath him, the tip of his cock grazing her slit. "No... You will *not* marry him!"

"Carson, it must be!"

"No!"

His eyes burned, a snarl curling along the edge of his lips, so passionate that she could do nothing else but listen to him when it mattered the most. She caught her breath, spellbound by his passion – she'd never seen this side of him! And maybe that side too was just what she was waiting to see as he hesitated, blushing, licking her muzzle with just the very tip of his tongue, a kiss that spoke volumes over any passionate embrace and exchanging of sloppy lust.

"I… I love you, Kasha."

And, with that, he slammed into her, sealing the deal and taking her virginity – his too, if he was being honest about it. Like she had saved herself for him, Carson too had kept himself pristine for her, although that could have been because he was too busy with his hunting endeavours and work for anything else, let alone dragonesses. No, Kasha was the only dragon for him and he kissed her neck over and over again, adoring her as she deserved to be adored.

Kasha's passage tightened around him as her heart soared, loving every last moment even as her body stretched and strained to accept him, passion rising and throbbing through even her mind. There was too much going on, one sensation coming hastily after the one that preceded it, and yet she had no wish or desire to call halt to anything as he thrust slowly and gently, allowing her body to grow used to the size of him after that first penetration.

She could not tell whether he was large or not, but she moaned out his name, crying softly for him to cover her, all the same. Her dress hung useless around her body but she would have cast it aside if she'd had the will to, only wanting him to keep thrusting, keep on powering into her, giving her every last dose of that pleasure that she all of a sudden seemed to crave so very badly. Her chest and flanks heaved, golden scales glittering in the tasteful, softening light, but he was not looking at her, eyes closed as the drake in question fought and fought to contain his pleasure.

Kasha's head spun – he had to be getting close already! Did she do that to him? Was she such an erotic creature that she could make such desire rise up in him like that? Whether or not it was so did not matter as she moaned for him, begging him to thrust into her harder, faster, to take her as a dragoness needed to be taken. And yet she could tease him too, her inner walls clenching and squeezing instinctively around that smoothly meaty shaft, heart pounding for the thrilling revelation that, finally, she had what she'd wanted in life. Maybe all along she'd known it was to be Carson, even if she'd never quite imagined the time to tell the tale to happen in her powder room of all places!

Oh, but how he made her heart leap and dance an irregularly lustful beat for him, clinging to him as if she was afraid that he was going to pull away too soon, muzzle tucked into his neck. The dragoness humped back at him with every ounce of strength and passion she had in her body, wanting him closer, but his scales were already pressed up to hers, the slit at the base of his belly that normally contained his cock brushing hers with each and every desperate stroke. And he truly was desperate with the fact that he simply could not hold back, snarling and panting like a demon, wings trembling and mantled over his back. What was it about her that made him want to cum so soon? It wasn't like masturbating in the privacy of his living quarters!

No… It was Kasha who awakened such driving desire in him and he caught her mouth again passionately with his, kissing her deeply as his tongue wound intimately around hers, their bodies joined in more ways than just the one. His cock curved up slightly, hitting a spot inside her that she had not known had existed, and Kasha tensed, eyes trying to close even as she sought to take in every last salacious drop of their intimacy at all costs, wings flapping (or trying to) beneath her back.

"C-Carson!"

That was all she got out as her first orgasm crashed over her, the storm unleashed in a peal of thunder and lightning, the roaring grumble snarling through as if a beast from the heavens had come down to show her just what the ways of love truly were. And there was no way either that a dragon like Carson would be able to hold back, heaving and panting, her passage rippling and massaging his hot length, coaxing him to spill his load as he was already so desperate to do.

But the physical pleasure was nothing compared to the emotional connection, her body beneath him, craving everything he had to offer and would give to her for the rest of their lives together, so very willingly. Breaking the kiss – it was sloppy in her howling of his name anyway – he clenched his jaws against a roar, loins tensing, everything hinging on one moment as he prepared to spend his seed.

The release, when it came, was in a rush, his cream hastening to seed her, a flood of cum surging through his aching shaft over and over again. And then the pleasure hit, sealing away his mind from the waking world and all the dragon could do was hump and thrust and hope that the erratic nature of it all was not too much for her, making him seem like an amateur where he wanted to be an expert.

Kasha wouldn't have noticed, that cum filling her up, spilling sloppily and deliciously out of her pussy. Her dress had not been salvageable before but the reek of his thick and musky cum made it all the worse and for the better too, her moan rising as she trembled, pleasure thrumming through her the aftershock of some manner of natural disaster. And yet all had to come to an end as he kissed her passionately and sweetly, breathing heavily as they came down from their joint high, his orgasm going on and on as he filled her to the brim and more with a hefty dose of his cum. Her body, after all, could hold far more but there was eroticism too to how it slicked from her, staining her scales and marking her irrevocably as his.

There would be no wedding to Davenport any longer.

"Carson?"

She smiled, batting her eyelashes at him even as he slunk his head back, shy even after everything.

"I love you too."

Their lips met in a tender kiss that meant so much more, bodies held together even as his cock softened. Time was fraught but it was only that trickster of time itself that would tell just what the future held for them. Together, that was.

Kasha's heart soared.

Always, together.

Paw Play

Verity groaned, the fennec fox's toes wriggling as she laid back on the sofa, though she was not alone there. With her pale tan fur, the points of her belly, chest and crotch a lighter shade than what would have been hit by the sun, if she had gone around in the nude on a daily basis, she was covered adequately if soft fur from head to toe – but not enough to be decent naked. The folds of her bare pussy could be just about seen between her legs as she let them lie together, softly with the tiniest gap between them, along the length of the sofa.

Her large ears twitched as she giggled, the TV on, though Verity had not honestly thought that she was going to be there for long. She had tucked herself well enough down against the back of it, against the cushions, that she could have gone undetected, her thick brush wiggling faintly. It swept back and forth lightly, only the base trapped under her rump, though she was quite comfortable where she was, entirely naked. The living room, if only that room, was more than warm enough for her, even if they had one of those funky systems that could only heat one room at a time. That had been the doing of her partner, however, in making sure that her home, while they were still dating, was as comfortable as possible for her.

The Gila Monster was a partner that not many would have expected to find her with, though Xavier had been smitten with her from the get-go. Of course, there had been the problem of his venom for them to contend with when they were in such close quarters with one another, but Verity thought they had more than managed things over the course of their one-and-a-half-year relationship with one another. With yellow patterning over his black, leathery body, he was a lizard, even if a venomous one – and they had been taking protective doses of anti-venom to both neutralise his venom and build up her resistance to it, so it would do no harm if anything went wrong.

Of course, that was something that most anthros did, so it was not a concern at all to either of them in starting their relationship; it was only the rare few that didn't take care of their venom and, even then, they'd often need to have it neutralised if it was deadly. But that wasn't something for either of them to worry about, not as Xavier, nude but for his boxer shorts, hunkered down on his belly in the living room doorway, knocking the door shut with this thick, black tail.

Verity giggled, though the Gila Monster couldn't see her ears poking up over the sofa, even if he knew well enough where she was hunkered down. Even with an anthro body, the reptile did not grow any hair at all, leaving his head a little bumpy, faintly so, from the natural "bead-like" texture of his skin, which was due to having a tiny bone under every scale there, giving him the texture. There were other lizards like that in the world but none over where he and Verity were studying at their university, though they were coming up to their final months before graduation, everything on track.

"Heh-he…"

He knew he wound her up sometimes, but the fox didn't seem like she was in a grumpy mood and his long tongue lashed out darkly, slapping against the side of his muzzle as the lizard scented the air.

"Oh no," she called out. "I hope a Gila Monster doesn't come and tickle my toes!"

He could have laughed aloud, but still managed to hold up the pretence and the play that he was going for. Of course, she knew he was there – and, still, her acting was terrible. But Verity didn't have to be anything of a good actor at all, no, not when it was the two of them together. Besides, she was studying Ancient

History and was already set up in a museum locally to work and kick start her career afterwards. He could have sat and listened to her talk about whatever interested her, any ancient history or even more recent history where new discoveries especially were being made, for hours upon hours.

Okay, so maybe Xavier was just a little infatuated with her, but that was not to be helped. Especially not as he slunk his way across the living room carpet, belly scales brushing the beige, though it was just rented accommodation. He would have preferred tiles or wood, but they couldn't be choosy when they were still at university together.

Yet she still laughed when his head appeared over the edge of the sofa where her hind paws were, so small and so delicate with the fluff poking out between her toes. That was an adaptation that, in ancient times, would have given her ancestors a better ability to withstand the heat of the desert. It could still be seen with the fennec foxes that had not developed like anthros of the world, though they could be a reclusive species sometimes too.

Verity giggled as Xavier's face appeared, his black-blue tongue flickering in and out with that sexy forked tip. She'd always liked that about him, though it had never been a defining feature at all of their relationship, no, not at all. Even though his yellow markings, signifying his venom, were striking. Everything about him just made her toes curl and her body sing with heat.

"Oh, no…" She murmured, lust rising within her, curling and twisting around the core of her being. "The monster has found me…"

He chuckled throatily, licking his lips with a wet smack as Xavier scented the air, need flowing through him, the edges of the slit that held his shaft back plumping up ever so slightly to part. But that could come later. After more than a little paw play for his cute vixen…

"And you know what that means…" He rumbled, though the words came out more ominously than Xavier would have intended. "You must submit to having your feet worshipped, cutie-fox. Prepare for no mercy!"

Okay, so perhaps he wasn't the best actor, but it was all worth it as he scuttled in and sensually curled up from the ground, as if the laws of gravity did not apply to the Gila Monster with the angle at which he curved his body. But he was only interested in licking her feet, in doing what she had covertly suggested to him at the beginning, his tongue dancing over and playing with the fluff of her hind paws. The fennec fox giggled and flinched away from him, though that was only a subtle reflex of her body and not something, to be fair to Verity, she could control. He would just have to apply more pressure then, to make sure that she knew he was there, that her body did not have to allow such ticklish sensations, from a fluttering, light touch to something deeper and more sensual.

Verity moaned as his tongue wormed its way thickly across her hind paw, her fingers clenching and tugging at her ears.

"Ohhhh, Xavier," she cried out softly, wriggling and squirming with a light yip on the sofa. "That feels… Mmmm!"

That was the best praise, to be fair, that she could have given him, however: being so struck with what little he had done to her so far that she was lost for words. Yet Xavier pressed on, his tongue providing her increased pressure, teasing and caressing over the top side of her toes, taking care to please both of her fluffy hind paws at once. It tickled briefly, but that sensation swiftly faded when he did the same as he had done before and increased the pressure, her fur dampening down slightly from what saliva there was lingering in his muzzle. There was not as much there as there would have been for a fox, though even fennec foxes did not waste water even when it was something that would better help them digest meals.

Without any fear of the lizard's bite, she wriggled and relaxed back into the sofa, splaying out her toes for him as, tenderly, Xavier took her right hind paw into his mouth, swirling his tongue around and around. At first, that had made her scared and shivery to have a predator like him almost devouring her little foot, yet, very swiftly, sensuality and the throb of arousal that it brought her overcame all else.

So, fear could be set aside in lieu of pleasure, even as she wriggled and splayed out her toes within his mouth. He did not do too much for her too soon, however, taking it at her own pace and making sure that the vixen was more than comfortable with everything he was doing. And yet Verity found herself completely unable to relax back down into the sofa while heat clawed at her, demanding that she pay her arousal its due attention, a tentative paw working its way down between her thighs to toy with and play along the edge of her pussy lips.

The Gila Monster was only somewhat aware of what his partner was doing, holding her leg carefully with his hands while he toyed with and sucked on her toes. The claws were short and thankfully blunt, though he could swirl and pull his tongue along her paws, dragging it through the fur, though that was quickly becoming soaked with even the limited dampness of his mouth. It was of no matter, even if he would lovingly tuck her into the bath after their fun together, swiping his tongue up along the fluffier underside of her paw that he had not yet reached.

Her foot extended up, the pads tender but fluff running up the back of her leg too, right up to her hock and beyond. The paws interested the Gila Monster the most, of course, but he still spared more than a few languid moments of attention on the longer part of her leg too, for it looked like it was a part of her paw when she had them tucked up like that so sweetly. Dragging his tongue all the way back down, he clamped his jaws playfully, mindful of his teeth, around her whole paw, rumbling around it and lashing the tip of each toe with his tongue.

Verity squealed and groaned, her body seemingly unable to decide whether it wanted rougher play or gentler touches, but Xavier was more than happy to give her both.

"Yes… Please…" She whimpered, all wide-eyed and pleading, her eyes even a little watery as she looked down at him, as if there was a part of the vixen that thought, even then, that the lizard would not give her what she and her body so desperately needed in that moment. "More… This makes me feel so good, Xavier, I… Please… Please lick my other foot. My toes too, all of my paw…"

He moaned around her, need rising, the thickness of his shaft finally sliding from the slit at the base of his belly. Oh, he was more than willing to do that, the urge to slide into her growing with every passing second; yet the Gila Monster was ready to please her.

He took his time with her other paw, though he paid it just as much, if not more, attention still, lashing his tongue sensually all around and making quite sure to drag it slowly between every toe, all four of them. The claws grazed his tongue, but he did not flinch, his eyes darkly adoring of her, even as need throbbed between his legs. His shaft hung down a little under its weight, not the kind of cock to spring up with its turgidity, but he did not mind that either. As long as he fit inside his gorgeous little vixen, the lizard only a couple of inches taller than her, it was all well in his mind.

Yet she was so small, so slight, his hands skilfully caressing past her paw and up her leg to her other hock as he suckled on her foot. It was so small in his mouth, so delicate, so fragile… And he was honoured that Verity trusted him with such an extreme act, for there were risks involved, especially with being in such close contact for such a long time. It would have been just the same, of course, if he was eating out her pussy, lashing his long tongue up inside her, but there was a tenderness in the gentleness of his bite, holding her faintly without ever the once digging his teeth in.

To do so would have broken her trust in him forever and Xavier could not have that, never.

Verity wriggled, panting more heavily. Oh, she was not going to last much longer, not with how she was plunging her fingers in and out of her pussy, trying to squeeze in a third digit to her sex. She needed him and yet she loved the slick feel of his tongue on her paw pads, when he could find them through her fur, the thick fluff more than enough to cover them most of the time. Yet he tickled her toes with a lighter touch and her black nose twitched, scenting his need on the air.

"Mmmm… Xavier… You need…"

She wanted him and yet could not find the words to tell the lizard just what she wanted from him, even though they were right there – right there on the very tippy-tip of her tongue! The fox whined and squirmed back and forth, knocking him lightly, though the Gila

Monster merely looked up at her, his eyes half-lidded with raw lust and need.

She swooned before him, melting into the cushions, her tail flicking back and forth madly as passion got the best of her. And yet the best she could do for herself was to wrench the hind paw that she was not having bathed with his glorious tongue away from him, spreading her legs wide as a result and pumping her hips up and down. It was awkward, mostly bearing up from one hind paw alone, but she managed it, brushing a thumb over her clit with a low cry.

"Xavier – please!"

He gave in to her in that moment too, though neither was truly in control of that situation, more so passing that very control back and forth between them so that the individual who was most suited to taking the lead was in control whenever they were needed. It was a mutual understanding, especially when it came to the sweet tenderness of paw play, but he had to scramble up then, letting her paw slip from his muzzle as his eyes burned with a lizard-like franticness.

He pressed over her, pinning her lovingly to the sofa as his jaws hung open, his thighs holding hers down and apart in a mating press. Of course, for the time being, the fox was on birth control – but the position still had a rather kinky name to it, a version of missionary where Verity's legs were held splayed out a little and apart so that his cock had an open invite to her pussy.

The fox squealed and tried, failing, to buck up against him, licking her lips – though nothing would have stopped that yowl from breaking free as his hot length ground up inside her. Xavier thrust into her pussy the first time, sliding in smoothly, and slammed in deeply and quickly, with urgent, shaky, juddery strokes of his cock. Oh, how he needed her, but the fennec fox tried to buck ardently up against him, even as pleasure crashed through her.

Her howl of ecstasy cut through the room, seeming to echo – though there were not all that many soft furnishings in there to dampen the sound. It gave the odd effect of apparently bouncing off the walls, but that did not stop the Gila Monster from thrusting and grinding into her still, needing her, her pussy, her body clenching and pulling around him. He snarled, jaws hanging open, his black-blue tongue lashing out, yet all was well as Verity climaxed on his cock, too close to the edge to even hold back for a single moment more.

That only left Xavier and he relished every moment of it, the soft, feminine taste of her paw still in his mouth as he swirled his tongue around, revelling in it. A little of her soft fur had come away too as she was moulting, shedding for the warmest months of the year, and clung to the end of his muzzle, tickling his nose. The lizard growled, leaning over her, his head tucked down close to the crook of her neck, every thrust bringing him closer and closer to the edge, until, finally it was all past the point of no return.

He growled, letting it roll through him, thick spurts of cum leaving his cock, so strong that every spurt seemed to come with a pause between it. Light-headed, he grunted into the crook of her neck, pressing down into her soft fur, loving it, lusting for it, though he could have done no better for himself at all after having his sweetheart, his girlfriend, under him, her pussy tight around his throbbing cock.

Yet that was all pleasure to be shared between them, lust and love in equal measures. He was already thinking of how he was going to take care of her that night, all the lovely things he was going to do for her – all because Verity deserved it. The fox stroked his head and neck gently, chirping to him in that little fox-ish squeak of hers, and he could not help but chuckle, nuzzling affectionately into her touch.

In a little paw play, they could learn even more about one another. And their lust left Xavier looking forward, with great pleasure, to all they could have next time too.

Always with kinky fun and love held close to their hearts.

Bound Bunny

"Mmmm..."

Reyna moaned, the black and white bunny squirming where she knelt, though she couldn't move really, not all that much. Although most furry species were mixed those days, her colouration spoke of a Dutch rabbit with the distinctive black and white colouration, with a white blaze down the centre of her face, covering her twitching nose and whiskers. She wriggled again, delighting in her restriction, though the red-furred wolf standing above her had a part in that too.

She blinked, enjoying the tightness of the soft bondage rope around her forearms, which crossed her arms behind her back, pressing her forearms together. Her legs had a spreader bar between the knees, smaller than one they'd tried between her ankles, which had the delicious effect of allowing her to walk — only if Fell helped her up.

The wolf growled, naked but for his natural fur, the lights in the bedroom turned down low as the different shades of red and brown were highlighted in his coat. Like most wolves, he had a softer, off-white front, the white stretching down his body from his chest, across his belly and dipping between his hind legs. There was a sliver of white on the underside of his tail too, but Reyna wasn't really looking at that, no, not when her eyes were locked onto the thickening swell of her boyfriend's sheath.

Well, Fell wasn't really her boyfriend, no, not at that time. Not when they were roleplaying, though they did not have specific roles, not like those that were more into the scene of domination and submission than they were. To Reyna, Fell was "Sir" when they were playing like that. So, that was all the bunny anthro had to remember.

And she knew she was safe there too, as he trailed his fingers up the line of her jaw, tilting her head up briefly as she let out a soft exhalation. Oh, Fell knew how to play her body and her emotions like an instrument, but they had a safe word too, which would be used if anything got too much for Rayna or even if she needed a little break. It was all okay and, frankly, things didn't need to be too serious in sex. As long as the safety boundaries were in place, neither the wolf nor the bunny had ever understood why people took things so intensely.

But maybe that worked for others. Not for them. Even if they were testing out more and more bondage, things that spiced up their sex life in a way that worked for them.

"Mmm, my pretty little bunny…"

Oh, how she loved the lazy drawl in his voice. It made her want to please him right there and then, but, in her bondage with her knees forced apart, all Reyna could do was wait until she was instructed and ordered to please. She whimpered softly, tipping forward after his retreating fingers, though Fell didn't allow her to suckle on them, not at that time. Maybe later…

"Do you want something?" He murmured, holding all the cards, even though she swayed there lightly, peering up at him from half-lidded eyes. "I think there's something a little thing like you can do for me."

"Mmm… Please…"

Reyna breathed out the words, though it felt natural to beg, panting softly, her lips parted. Maybe that was something she could try another time too.

The wolf grinned, rocking back on his heels as Fell allowed his natural lust and inclinations to rise, throbbing through him lightly, though it was anything but soft. Perhaps "rhythmic" would have been a better way to phrase it, the wolf shifting his weight back and forth as he ran his fingers down and around his sheath.

Yet why ever would the wolf had had to do any more than that when he was there with his beautiful bunny was beyond him. He cupped her face and let Reyna moan, tipping her cheek into his touch, his shaft pulsing, slowly but surely sliding from the fleshy, soft pocket of his sheath. It filled out from the base as a pink length pushed out, the tapered tip stretching into the air.

He took note of his partner, sweet in her submission, tip towards him, though Reyna still waited. She didn't have to, but she wanted to try, wanted to see where submission could lead her – while Fell took control instead.

The wolf inhaled, folding his fingers around the base of his cock and pumping the length of it, up and down, slowly coaxing it to full hardness even though his dick did not need all that much convincing. All the while, the wolf's eyes did not leave the bunny for a single moment, not as he salaciously licked his lips and ran his tongue deviously along the outside of his muzzle.

"Mmmm…"

"Oh… Please…"

Reyna's eyes didn't leave his cock as she locked on to him, squirming again, rocking back and forth. She knew there were safety scissors to cut the ropes, if ever needed, but the bunny still pulled deviously against their restriction, taking short little panting breath after breath, dragging what airs she could into her lungs. Reyna was not all that sure how she knew, but there was a part of her, even in that moment, that knew she would need it.

"Now, my sweet," he breathed, letting Reyna hang on his every word. "Come here… You know what to do with that beautiful, soft mouth of yours."

Oh, and how the bunny did! In an instant, she'd tipped forward, neatly closing the distance between them as if it had never been, moaning faintly as she took his length into her mouth. Her lips folded succulently around the head of his cock and the wolf did not even need to draw her down further on his hot length, trembling with need within her mouth, though Reyna took her time.

She was not, after all, there to rush through the experience, but to please him. He was her "Sir" and she wanted to make sure Sir felt as good as he could.

In a way, it meant she could simplify her life too, so that she didn't have to make the big decisions there, though there was still room for initiative when she was unbound. Sometimes even within the realm of being bound too, though that took ingenuity.

So, she used that ingenuity, cupping his cock on her soft, flexible tongue. She drew her tongue up along the underside of his length as she sucked lightly on him, her cheeks hollowing faintly as she increased the pressure. Part of that was merely for show but, well…she could do things just for show too, so she drove her partner wild, thrusting and humping and grinding. Yet she doubted fell would ever quite be out of his own control, for that was something the wolf held a rigid grasp on, despite everything.

In dominating, she knew, he took back some of the control he didn't feel he had in the rest of his life. Therein lay the difference between them and, perhaps, that was why they fit so well as partners and in the bedroom too.

But that was not for Reyna to delve into, not at that moment. The rest of the world, even the soft, comfortable bedroom she knew so well, fell away as if it had no matter at all to her anymore. The smooth flesh of his cock sliding against her lips and tongue was inviting, perhaps a little too much so, and she finally closed her eyes, letting the moment wash over her.

The heat of her wolf played deep and she groaned faintly, ears twitching. Her knees still needed to stay apart, though that was all by the by as far as she was concerned, swaying a little though confident Fell would catch her if ever needed. She didn't quite feel balanced there, but that was okay.

She wasn't meant to be in control. She was meant to be there, submissive to him. And that meant she didn't have to think at all.

Oh, and what a relief that was! To not think, to let her world suck down into the pressure of her lips around his cock and letting how good that simply felt, all on its own, roll through her, thrust after thrust and stroke after stroke. Reyna groaned around Sir's cock, slipping lower and lower, her black ears flicking and smoothing back, even though they would have normally been perked and in an upright position.

That didn't matter, no, not in that moment… She murmured around his cock as the wolf dominantly put a commanding paw on the back of her head and thrust, sliding into her mouth again and again with every long, sensual rock of his hips. The bunny trembled before him, trying to do all she could with her tongue, cradling that thick length of wolf meat, but there was nothing really Reyna needed to do, oh no.

Just be there. Just be pretty. Just be simple. Just be *sweet*. And it was oh so very sweet as Fell growled, tipping forward over her, filling her mouth, grunting softly as he thrust.

He wasn't losing control, oh no, not when the wolf was the one too who very much needed to be there and in control, his muzzle wrinkling slightly as he huffed and panted. Oh, but Reyna made it all so difficult to keep that control at all times, even if they were safe there. He slid one of her ears between his fingers, gripping them lightly, though he knew not to tug too hard. No, that would come along with some rougher play for them both, if that was something too that they chose to explore.

It was just too divine to slide into her mouth, the smooth purse of her lips sealing tightly around his throbbing length. Fell grunted, admiring her even though his knot threatened to swell too quickly, letting the carnal moment wash over him.

When he was with Reyna, like that, it didn't really feel like they were still there, in the bedroom, no, not at all. It was like being transported to another time and place, somewhere everything fit just right, nothing clunky or awkward about it at all. Of course, there were still some tricky points to sex and the focus on safety in BDSM kept them secure in their play: for them, it was exactly as they needed. And it made sure they were set to carry on, regardless of whether a scene went perfectly or had some juddering moments to it.

"Mmmm... My sweet bunny..." He crooned. "Take it all, every inch."

Reyna grunted, her eyelids fluttering. Oh, but it was so much! Her cheeks already filled out with his cock, trying to take him all, even though that didn't really help him slide into the back of her mouth and throat. Her head bobbed on his shaft as she groaned and gulped around him, her eyes watering, though Reyna didn't need to let the tears flow softly down her cheeks. If anything, they were tears of happiness, though the strain sometimes of taking a cock as big as her Sir's into her mouth was a challenge in itself.

"Mmmph... Nngghhh..."

She drifted, sucking on his cock, trying to do as he wanted her to. She just had to take a little more, just a little more, into her mouth, sucking it all down, her cheeks hollowing again as she increased the pressure around his cock.

And yet Fell took matters into his own paws, pinching softly at the base of her ears to draw her forward. Reyna eagerly followed his leading paw and gulped, her throat bulging as she fought to take him down, though it was always a challenge to gulp down a cock as big as Fell's.

That was no matter, no matter at all… She would take it, of course, all as she had before, her eyes watering again. The bunny groaned around his cock, a trickle of drool slipping from the corner of her lips, yet she didn't concern herself with it. A little mess was normal, perfectly so, and she huffed through her nostrils, dragging in all the air she could while she savoured Sir's cock.

Above her, the wolf grunted and she let a little tremor roll through her, sweet in the knowledge she was getting to him. Oh, how she was getting to him… That was a good thing, a very good thing, and Reyna bobbed her head, pulling against his paw, so wrapped up in trying to devour his cock with her soft, succulent mouth she was barely aware of being out of rhythm with Fell.

He eased off, however, better able to settle and adjust with her lips smooth and soft along the length of his cock. Fell couldn't let his knot swell, no, not yet. He had to ease through the moment, to let it come, bit by bit, huffing and grunting, his ears twitching while Fell strained to control himself the best he could.

There, however, was only so much a wolf could do about that and, at some point, Fell had to remove his shaft from the deviously delightful source of stimulation entirely.

"Mmmm!"

Reyna whined and cast him a sullen look as his cock pulled from her mouth, leaving a string of saliva, perhaps with a little pre-cum mixed into it too, though that didn't bother her. She just wanted the musky, lustful taste of her wolf back in her mouth where it belonged, serving him devoutly, with nothing else mattering.

"Mm," she grunted, pushing up on her knees a little more, tail bobbing and twitching faintly. "Please… Sir… More…"

"Ah-ah, my lovely little bunny," Fell said with a wolf-ish grin. "Don't you want a better filling? Come here."

Reyna quivered, though she wasn't really able to get up or do anything on her own. That meant it was down to her wolf to check the curtains were drawn all the way, the soft, low light from the lamp on the bedside table illuminating the scene, though the bunny felt she would have known exactly where the wolf was, regardless of whether the lights were left on or not.

But she liked seeing him above her, cutting a dark, striking figure, muscle showing lightly through his fur, even though his fur softened the edges of his frame and the outline. That was just something about having fur that no one would ever get along with, where the detail and definition of their bodies often were different to what showed outwardly.

But she knew how he was, wanting to curl her fingers around the muscles in his arms, to feel him pressed up to her. Yet all Reyna could do was rise as he helped her up by her hips. The bunny blinked as she caught the little quirk of a smile about the wolf's lips.

He's enjoying this… She thought with a shiver. *How helpless I am…*

But that was okay too. As long as she was there, forever and always, with her wolf.

Fell laid her on the bed, on all fours – kind of. With her arms bound behind her back, the bunny could not support her chest, so he merely slid a pillow under her, so she was just about at the right angle. No more than that needed to be done, her knees kept apart from him, her buttocks at just the right height for Sir to tease.

And, oh, how Fell could have teased her, lapping and slurping up into her hot, wet sex just to remind her of the position she was in, the control he had over her, completely and utterly. Reyna squirmed softly against the ropes, testing the limits of them all over again, but they held her fast, just as she wanted, rubbing over her forearms as they were kept against her back.

"Ohhhh, please…"

She moaned softly, adjusting her weight so she was a little more comfortable. Yet Reyna didn't want to be fully comfortable, no, not with the restrictions in play and in place. She was there to be bound, to have so much taken out of her control, moaning faintly, for she didn't know with what words she wanted to beg.

It was better to whimper as he knelt behind her, the head of his firm shaft easing into her pussy lips. Reyna tried to wriggle, but the softness of the mattress meant she couldn't really rock back on to his cock, rendered sweetly helpless all over again, her toes flexing and curling alternatingly.

Yet the bunny was right where she wanted to be, hissing through her teeth and puffing out her cheeks with air, losing herself right there, in a moment that was hers and hers alone.

That was okay… She didn't have to think. Not as Fell whispered her name and slowly sank every inch of his cock into her. He stretched her out, bit by bit, as her pussy hugged the full girth of his shaft as if she was trying to draw him deeper, so very much so. The wolf too, her dominant of the moment, was right where he needed to be, grinding in slowly, surely, letting her pussy stretch around him so she could take more of his cock, grunting softly as he tried, even then, to restrain his need.

"Mine…"

Fell growled lustfully and Reyna quivered, though the bunny was rather wrapped up in the sensation of being penetrated. She didn't have to say anything in return, not as she inhaled and exhaled softly, her sides fluttering and juddering with breath, for it did not feel, not even then, that it came easily. Maybe it was never meant to as she did her best to clench around him, to give her Sir even more pleasure than her hot pussy already was.

"Mmmm… I love it when you do that, sweet bunny…" Fell groaned, the wolf licking his lips. "So… Do it again for me."

"Mmmph!"

Reyna was ready to oblige as Fell thrust, grinding the full length of his cock in and out as he found the rhythm and pace that suited him. Her body was merely a toy at his disposal, even though Reyna was lucky indeed that Fell cared about her pleasure too. Her body ached and tingled as he used her, but the bunny had little idea how hard she was squeezing around his cock or even if Sir could feel it when he thrust like that.

Every stroke of his cock into her ground deep, his hips bouncing off her buttocks, and she moaned aloud, relishing in the moment, losing her sense of self.

She didn't need to hold on to it, revelling in the pure nature of sensation alone, the bonds on her arms tight, so wonderfully so.

"Mmmph! Mmm… Sir, please!"

Fell tipped forward over her, holding on to her hips, though that was as much to hold himself in the moment as it was to dominate her. The smallest of things often had bigger effects than even he could anticipated and the wolf had spent rather a lot of time experimenting with that when it came to Reyna. Even then, she peered back at him, as if she was trying to make sure he did not see her, still trying to be covert and discreet in how she snuck a quick glimpse of him.

Yet she was so sweet under him, in her black and white fur, her ears splaying down softly, relaxing as he took her. Fell growled, letting her see the sheen of saliva on his teeth and the lash of his pink tongue across his lips, before she trembled back around again, her chest pinned to the pillow, shuddering bodily as he took her.

His knot swelled and, that time, the wolf didn't even have to tease her clit to get her off, not when his knot was already doing a good job of pulling through her pussy as it bloated and thickened. The pull of it set off something carnal in Reyna and the bunny squirmed on his cock, teased to the brink of losing control.

Yet it was for Fell to push her over the edge as he seated himself deep inside her and thrust in short, sharp, desperate strokes of his cock. His knot ground back and forth within her – but never left her pussy, no, not as it inflated inside her. It locked their bodies together, kept there through the tie, tugging resolutely at her sex while he pulled back, testing just how closely their forms were kept there.

Fell growled, licking his lips. There was no backing out from that point, the delicious sense of impending orgasm calling him on and on. He had to heed it, even if he could have stilled, with a very great effort of will, and allowed his knot to deflate inside her, her pussy gripping him so very tightly.

Yet neither wolf nor bunny wanted that, oh no, not as he thrust harder and faster, grinding his hips into her backside at a truly fervent pace. The bunny whined and grunted as he powered into her, until a breathless squeal nigh on ripped itself from her lips as she cried out, orgasm taking her. Her pussy clenched around him, tighter than ever before, but there was only so much she could do as waves of climax rolled through her, again and again.

Reyna moaned, her ears twitching, her dominant partner the only thing that grounded her, keeping her there in the moment where she belonged. She rocked her hips weakly back against him, though barely moved at all, her hamstrings aching from the position she'd been forced into and how hard she braced against it.

"Mmm, my lovely bunny..." Fell breathed, though his voice was hoarser and raspier than before. "You feel so good on my cock..."

She whined, but he relaxed there, letting the rock of his body carry him forward. With every stroke, he plunged his shaft as deeply inside her as he possibly could, panting heavily, long, rasping breaths dragging in through an open mouth. The wolf, however, could not hold out forever, not as his knot swelled to its thickest, plumpest extent, tying their bodies in place, grinding in hard as he stifled a howl.

And then Fell let it out, his throat trembling with the force of his cry, finally releasing inside her. They didn't need a condom when they had already agreed that there was no need for one in their relationship and there was a divine sense of flesh-on-flesh contact that Fell longed for each and every time.

Yet it was all about Reyna under him, how his bunny quivered as she was filled, his cock letting loose hot spurts of cum inside her. He hoped he'd pull out, when his knot finally deflated, to a thick, messy cream-pie of cum spilling from her pussy. But that would only be seen in fifteen minutes or so, something like that, after his knot softened enough to lightly tug free. It was always something they had to contend with in sex, which had both good points and bad points to it.

Fell leaned down close to her and Reyna relaxed into the wolf's warmth, how it sank into her body. He was all she needed, all she longed for, at peace after the high of climax, letting a soothing glow seep softly through her veins.

In the sweet release of submission, she could have it all, from the tight pressure of his knot swelling within her pussy to the comforting press of his fur to her glutes and lower back. Fell crooned her name, raspy and breathless, and she whispered back to him, wanting her lover to know she was there for him too.

"Fell… Sir…"

Right then, they were connected, closer than ever in physical form and emotional intimacy. And that was the way it needed to be for them, exploring and loving one another more and more every day.

Even if that meant, sometimes, Reyna was a bound bunny, just for her Sir.

Always, for him.

Six Studs & a Dragoness

Sapphire's eyes glittered as the blue dragoness knelt in the ring of males, the room around her tantalisingly dark, though the hues of her blue scales shifted with the light, sometimes a deeper shade and more mysterious with lighter, sparkling notes. She was a mystery with her long, elegant muzzle and dancing eyes, the way her horns appeared to have been softly carved with the brush of an artist, delicately shaped by fingers that knew what they were doing. Wide hips and a full chest took precedence on her figure and she was coveted by all.

Yet Saph enjoyed a very particular kind of intercourse… Namely, one where all the attention was on her, even though it was the guys that thought they were getting the better end of the deal.

She moaned.

The dragoness always got the best out of them.

"Yeah, boys, come on in…"

Sapphire was in her favourite dungeon room at the fetish club, a place where fantasies could be brought to life in the best of ways. There was nothing non-consensual there as she slurped up another dragon's cock, taking it into the back of her mouth while the dim lighting in there still managed to lend an air of mystery to it. She moaned around him, taking him deep, loving his paws on the back of her head, how he held her, as eager as ever to dominate her.

"Oh, yeah," he growled above her, though she did not know the silver drake's name. "That's the stuff… Take it all down, baby."

Maybe Saph had fucked him before and maybe she had not. It didn't matter to her, not when she had a hard cock in her maw, others in her paws. She stroked and teased them, hot lengths of gryphon and dragon meat – her favourite! Though there was a phoenix in the mix too, resplendent in glorious, rich, sunset feathers, along with a manticore.

She was most interested in him, to be fair, for she had never had a manticore fuck her, a tiger anthro with a scorpion tail that could harm, but, of course, had a cap on it for such activities. Although he could not turn the natural rhythms of his body that produced venom off, he could ensure that those around them were safe. There were usually antidotes around for that sort of thing too, but simply knowing how strong he was with his broad, powerful chest and shoulders made her heart tremble in the best of ways.

He had horns too, though they pointed back, not all that obvious, further denoting him as a creature like the dragons and gryphons, even the phoenix. They stepped about the wiles of normal anthros, though that was something that so very often meant that usual sexual activities didn't quite do it for them either, which could be a shame at times.

They had to push the boat out, had to seek out what made their hearts pound more than ever. And that was just why Sapphire was down on her knees before them, the six studs in total. Dragons and gryphons, three dragons, one gryphon, then topped by the manticore and phoenix, their dicks hard and proud, dripping with pre-cum already.

She could not help herself, forgoing the dragon for another as she rocked onto all fours, dragging the phoenix down with her. The avian squawked, but the others there knew how things went, clearly, and helped him down to his knees, the floor padded under her, but Saph didn't have it in herself to care just where she was kneeling. All she knew was the fire in her veins, how her heart pounded more fervently, a driving beat that coursed through her, pump after pump.

The phoenix's cock was coaxed into her maw, tongue curling hungrily around it, pre-cum dripping and drooling from the tip. He couldn't stop it, even as the others jostled him and told him to get on with it. Maybe he was new, but she'd show him the way – especially as a thick dragon with power in his back end knelt behind her.

"How're you doing, Saph?"

She didn't have the chance to answer as he plunged a fat length of uncut cock into her pussy, driving deep, her body welcoming him in as he fed her his dick. It drove deep, stretching her open, yet her body was used to it, used to him, a dick that she must have taken many times before, though it was not present in her memory. So many dicks all tended to blur into one mass of pleasure after a time, though she lusted for the penetration, the stretch and the drive of him anyway.

The big green dragon, built as if he was into bodybuilding, though with a thicker gut due to his age, knew what she liked: long strokes of his cock where his hips slapped her backside with every thrust. He had to be rough with her, for the dragoness would merely swap to someone else that she liked better if he was not good enough, the slutty, gangbanged dragoness accepting nothing at all less than the best. She grunted, taking the phoenix's cock deeply, her teeth kept carefully away from his cock, though it was ever so tempting, from time to time, to show them a little bit of teeth, just to remind them who held the power there.

The phoenix murmured as he humped her mouth, though she didn't mind someone that was shyer, as long as they got into it too. And he had that in him as he thrust and panted, his little tongue fluttering within his beak, though she knew that all avians like him breathed through their nares.

The manticore rumbled, pushing in, his cock on her shoulder as he jostled for his turn, uncut and the skin sliding back and forth, though she wanted more than that, so many cocks, ploughing her in every hole. Her fantasies ran amok as she tensed and howled around the phoenix's dick, letting him take over thrusting for the moment, for Sapphire could no longer bob her muzzle on his cock when orgasm was ripping through her. It stripped her brutally from the present and rooted her there too at the same time, opposing courses of action that shouldn't have matched.

Yet the pulses of pleasure running rampant through her body were not to be contested as the drake plunged into her, each shuddering thrust rocking her forward. Oh, how she wanted it – yet she was getting exactly what she craved right there at that very moment. Saph grunted and groaned, head spinning, completely and utterly overwhelmed with sensation. It did not even register with her that the lights in the room had gone even dimmer, rendering the moment steamier still in a mass of studly male bodies, all who wanted a piece of her to fuck.

The dragon snarled and she imagined his tongue hanging out as his balls slapped against her pussy as he thrust and thrust, demanding completion. His cock ploughed deeply up into her as he bellowed out a throaty orgasm, cum spilling inside her, though he did not stop thrusting for even one moment in the heat of orgasm.

She liked that. She liked that rather a lot, in fact.

It was hot and it was heady and it was everything that she wanted to be. Suckling on the phoenix's cock, more with her senses, she wrapped her tongue around and around him, her cheeks hollowing softly with the force of her suckling, until he could bear it no longer either. To render the flow of cum into her maw and down her throat was a thrill to be held in high regard – at least, that was how Saph saw it. The dragoness craved that manner of spine-tingling use more than anything else and she'd be damned if she wasn't going to get it for herself too.

She had to have it. There was no other option for her, not then, not ever.

She moaned, the phoenix cumming hard into her maw, jets of cum pouring down her throat at such a rate that she was glad that his long spire was crammed into the back of her throat as she wouldn't have otherwise been able to swallow it all. Mm, it was good, so fucking good, to get a cock like that, a male like that. Why, the only thing that could have made the phoenix better for her would have been if he'd had externally held testes, throbbing and pulsing, his need more obviously coursing through.

"Come here, slutty dragoness…"

It was her name, a collar around her neck and a tag denoting that, jingling whenever she was moved. In there, she was not just Sapphire or Saph but "slutty dragoness," the dragoness whore who was there to please every one of them over and over again. She grunted as she was hefted up in the air, a male before her, groaning as his cock pressed into her. Her chest pressed to his, though he was bigger than her, a gryphon with a shocking yellow beak and intelligent eyes, though there was nothing intelligent about the moan that slipped from his beak.

Sex made everyone dumb. It made them lack that sense of thinking and she loved the carnal nature of it, how it rendered them less and more than what they were, at the same time. It made them more feral and she wrapped her legs around the gryphon's brown-feathered hips, where they teased down into tan hips and thighs, to keep herself in place.

Yet that was not to be all of it as the manticore that she had so lusted for pressed in behind her, demanding what her body could give him. His dick was rounded rather than tapered and pushed into her asshole, straining to ease in with only his pre-cum for lube. But Sapphire was a skilled dragoness and a single cock like that was not truly going to cause her any issues as she allowed gravity to help, sinking down, catching her breath, her chest fluttering with lust.

"Oh, yeah..." She groaned, her voice deep, head rolling back onto the manticore's shoulder, his fur soft against her and muscles hard. "Fuck me... Fuck my slutty tail hole..."

He growled but had no more to say, bracing on both hind paws, his tail curling back and forth as excitement laced his body. He didn't want to have control any more than she did, for the expression of their sexuality was in losing control. Two male bodies pinned her on each side, their cocks firmly pressing up against one another through the barrier of flesh between her two holes, her passages aching, demanding more.

And Sapphire would have her more too as she moaned, climaxing on both dicks at once, her head thrown back, panting heavily, clinging to whoever seemed best at any given moment. Lust swarmed her like an infestation that simply could not be shaken off, need pumping through her bones.

"Yes," she breathed, though she was hardly sure they heard her at all. "More, fuck me, take me, breed me..."

She hadn't used protection. Of course, she hadn't. Sapphire never did and that was most likely why she'd laid so many clutches of eggs. Something in her, however, kept her coming back for a breeding gangbang, no one ever knowing whether the eggs inside her were viable or not.

They didn't need to know. Not as they served her needs.

She grunted thickly in the back of her throat, need pulsing through her, desire impossible to ignore, whimpering, moaning. The stretch of two dicks inside her was too much, even though she could take more, perhaps even more than one dick in each hole. It was enough, and that was all that mattered. It was enough to make her head spin and her heart pound, her moans rising and rising, even with the thickly masculine grunts of all the other males in the room with her.

"Yes…

"Such a good fuck…

"Slutty cock-sleeve…

"Fill her up!"

It was like a siren call to breed her, the gryphon and the manticore thrusting and grinding, the gryphon's keening cries bouncing off the walls. He was not one to hold off from his orgasm, or so she suspected, ropes of creamy cum flooding her pussy, adding to the load already in there, though her ass was still "dry" of its first load.

"Unff…" The gryphon moaned, bearing heavily into her as he shuddered through the aftermath of climax. "So…fucking hot."

He pecked her lightly on the cheek as he left her, the gryphon version of the kiss, the manticore grunting, groaning, though it was the exertion of his muscles that had him making such noises as, slowly, he lowered her to the ground. There, he could bear into her on all fours, taking her doggystyle once more. Sure, it had been done before, but there was pleasure to be had in cramming every inch of his meaty cock into her, ramming deep and hard, thrusting and grinding.

"Come on, dude…"

Unfortunately, the others didn't quite see it that way as they egged the manticore on to lie down on his back, leaving her drooling pussy open for use. It was a dragon that slotted in neatly between her thighs, the fifth one to take her, sliding in easily, for she had already been more than stretched out and loosened up for them.

She moaned, so full, so heavy, feeling the flow of cum up deeper and deeper inside her, squirming on two cocks at once. Sapphire needed more, so much more, yet she was in such a position that the dragoness had to trust them to give her that more, exactly as she demanded it. Her body yearned for it as they slammed into her, the manticore planting his feet and driving up, pound after pound of his cock slapping wetly up into her as his balls bounced off her arse.

"Grrr," he rumbled against the back of her head, somewhere above it. "So tight… Knew this was a good…unff…time to come for a fuck…"

For Sapphire was a dragoness very much in demand every time she came by to please herself at the fetish dungeon, her mind rising and falling on waves of lust so steep that she barely knew what was an orgasm and what was merely ecstasy. Everything seemed to blur into one snarling wrench of lust after a while, her cries rolling forth, need pulsing through, all so very desperately, so needfully.

The manticore tensed, thrusting hard, his cock feeling as if it was swelling, though that could not be so, not quite as she imagined it. Her chest heaved, need rising, yet her head had been tipped all the way back, the final dragon of the six studs pushing into her maw and throat. He was big, really big, her throat bulging out to take him, obviously swelling with the meat of his member driving there.

Around his cock, she hacked and gagged delightedly, relishing in the moment. There was nothing as carnal as being gangbanged, seeing so many males all around her, wanting her, craving her. She was the kinkiest thing in the room, splattered with cum, the males who were not currently engaged in fucking her jacking off, as if the mere sight of her naked, lustful body was too much for them to bear.

With three holes of her body filled, stuffed to bursting point, the dragoness was right where she wanted to be, her heart surging, pussy contracting and rippling erratically through yet another orgasm. The muscular tensions in her body could not be controlled and neither did she want them to be as the two dragons standing over her, using her body as nothing more than holes to be filled, swore and rammed in.

"Jeez, so close…"

"I'm gonna fucking blow…"

She had to have them all, every drop of cum that they had to give her. Some said that Sapphire was greedy, but she was merely a dragoness who knew what she liked, what she wanted, as the manticore bellowed out a roar under her. His cock throbbed and jerked within her as if the power of his orgasm was too much, her tail thrust off to the side, the tip curling back and forth with raw need. His cum flowed up into her, not a drop able to escape with the tightness of the seal of her ass around his cock, pumping deeper and deeper, her lower abdomen feeling fuller and tighter with every passing second.

"Ohhhh…"

She moaned, in a muffled fashion, around the dragon dick in her mouth, though she could not lap and slather him with too much attention in such a position. It didn't matter though as the dragons leaned over her fiercely, exchanging looks, trying to hold out for as long as possible, even though that wasn't really something that could happen when the dragoness under them was keening out in heat.

What Sapphire wanted, she got – and that was just how the dragons joined her in orgasm, cumming together, one filling her maw and the other adding to the load in her pussy. Who knew whether she would fall pregnant with yet another clutch of eggs from that breeding, but Saph was sure, either way, that she would have something to add to her collection after that exceptionally kinky night.

The slurp and slop of cum in her maw, flowing under her tongue and around her teeth was alluring as she gasped, the male drawing back, only to paint her face with his cream. She moaned, breathless and still wanting, the stud trembling in her pussy staying as still as possible, muscles braced and shaking.

"Take it easy there," she hissed, eyes alight with passion. "Don't want to wear you out too soon, my new toys. I can go all night. Can you?"

There was a challenge in her tone and she grunted, a cock suddenly pushed into her paw. That, of course, was the gryphon, more than up for the challenge while cream dripped down her face, marking her neck, Sapphire's lips breaking into a grin.

"I see someone can."

She'd have them all, again and again, until they all collapsed into a breathless, exhausted pile of lust, everyone satisfied – multiple times. Sapphire wouldn't have had it any other way, finally with a set of studs that she thought might just be able to keep up with her.

When she was done with them, there'd be others waiting in the wings anyway. She smirked, licking cum off the side of her muzzle, body resplendent with need, scales practically glowing in the low light.

Everyone wanted their time with the slutty dragoness, after all…

Worshipping Her Stud

"You're so strong…and your balls…"

Theresa whimpered, the submissive feral dragoness plaintively rubbing her head against her "master" dragon's nuts, moaning, whimpering, lowlier than she had ever been before him. Her pink scales glittered as if they had been sprinkled with moondust, a beauty of her species, though her dominant partner towered over her, twice her size and as lustful as her to boot.

Her elegantly curved horns, light and delicate, could not match up to the power of his huge ones that were like those of a ram, the kind of dragon who spent more of their time on the ground than under it, huge and bulky. Yet Alister's power was not to be denied as he rumbled a growl, the green and brown drake drabber in colour than her and yet so easily dominant that he made her legs buckle…

The forest closed in around them, dark and sultry, an enchanted kind of twilight that was tainted by their lust – or made better in the purple glow, fireflies dancing in shades of blue, flitting back and forth. They had their own passion to spend there, though it was of the adult kind, his hard, throbbing member pinkly demanding her attention, pre-cum spilling viscously. It was as if Theresa had made her way to the source of the creek, where it bubbled up from the mountainside, yet she could not wait to drink straight from the source.

She would have collapsed at his feet if not for the fact that she was already bowed down under him, Alister rumbled out a growl, her name on his lips.

"My pet…" He said, the deep boom of his voice sending a shiver down her spine. "Is there no more that you can do to show your love and devotion to my balls?"

A game, all part of their game. Outside of mating, they were equals in life and love, though the dominance and submission of their mating games… Oh, they had Theresa coming back time after time again.

His huge balls though… They were different. Unlike with other dragons, the kinds that spent more of their time and lives airborne, they swung under his body, a weight to them that could not be denied, throbbing, aching, desperate for her touch. That was a dragoness' joy and privilege, all in the act and the art of pleasing him, crooning submissively as she rubbed her elegant muzzle against his nuts.

"The musk of you…" She moaned aloud, tongue dangling from her mouth, lapping up against his nuts. "Master… It's so thick, I know how badly you want to fuck me. Please… Please, take your toy."

But she was down there to worship his nuts as the larger stud dragon rumbled above her, in a way that she hoped was approving. His musk washed over her, for dragons did not sweat, though there were scent glands between the smaller, more vulnerable scales around their genitalia and notably their anal rings too, under their tails. That could exude a deviously delightful concoction of scents to drive any dragoness wild with need, her tail lifting, the vent of her sex plush and full, swollen, even then.

She wanted him, was desperate for him, though all she could do was breathlessly whisper to her master how much she adored him, how she wanted him to fuck her again, to take her again. How she wanted that huge spear of his cock slamming into her, abusing her body, taking her as his. There was no other claim that Theresa ever wanted to be laid over her than Alister's, the studly, dominant dragon overpowering her with such ease that he made her swoon.

The forest floor met her forelegs damply as she bowed down under him, nuzzling at his cock, her long tongue slopping around him, giving him the messiest, lewdest blowjob that he could ever have wanted. It was crude and it was lewd, moaning as if she could not hold back, dipping her tongue into the slit of his sheath strained taut around the base of his cock. That was the muskiest still, though more from containing his cock than any specific scent glands, her head swirling with passionate lust as his scent clawed its way into her nostrils.

"Master… Please…" She begged. "Please fuck me, breed me, make me your slutty little dragoness toy for your monster balls…"

Perhaps not the sexiest thing to say to another, but they had been together for so long that they knew and understood one another, their little kinks, their biggest quirks. Alister rumbled above her, shifting his weight, bracing his hind legs, the huge length of his throbbing member pulsing out more pre-cum again, more than most males would deliver in orgasm.

She moaned, nuzzling into him, lapping up what she could, though she let it splash onto her muzzle, marking her scales as his, always his. One more little thing that she could do for her loving master, all for him, heat coursing through her.

Oh, how she needed to be fucked, to be filled, to feel his thick meat stretching her out while her pussy ached around him. The strain, of that first thrust, would always catch her off guard, even as she spared another moment in the worship of his balls, pressing into them, tenderly lapping, nuzzling, feeling the weight of his seed within.

It belonged inside her, spilling out of her pussy, so much that her womb and her cunt simply could not contain it all. There were no words for how hungry the dragoness was for his cum, every fervent beat of her heart pumping blood to all the right places of her body, her tail lifted to the point that she doubted that she could pin it down again. She was too hot, too needy, her sex burning up from the inside out. Even the scent of her pussy was thick in the air, hanging around them like a cloud of pheromones that neither drake nor dragoness could wriggle out of.

Desire. It claimed every fibre of their beings, lustfully so, her hips rocking back, wanting to grind onto his cock, even as the drake lowered his head, curling back around behind his foreleg so that he could tease her pussy. It was tricky, with the size difference, but at least the long necks of dragons came in useful sometimes – more often than not. His tongue lashed over her vent and tail hole in tandem, not caring whether he licked more of one than the other for she was perfectly clean back there, the heat of her body guiding him to where he needed to be. That was, of course, for teasing her, for riling his sexy bitch of a dragoness into a fervour.

There was nothing quite like seeing her mindless and mad with lust, after all, for Alister.

Theresa squealed, taking his cock into her long maw just for something to focus on, other than pleasure swamping her, her pussy dripping fluidly, marking her hind legs even as she spread them, bracing for her master. Oh, his tongue… His tongue could do such wonderful things to her, squirming up inside, though he more than knew how to find that pleasurable patch of nerves within her sex. He knew how to tease her, to drag her squalling to an edge of pleasure repeatedly.

She needed to get off, her body aching for it as much as she did for the hot length of his cock, though the dragoness hardly knew what she needed more, moaning and grunting, drooling around his cock. It had taken her many months, when they had first got together, for her to take Alister's dick fully, for he stretched out her throat with every thrust. They had got there in the end and there was nothing like the sensation of her throat swelling and bulging out to accommodate him, cutting off her ability to breathe as she swallowed him down.

Each gulp of her throat gave him more pleasure, the drake circling her tail hole with his tongue, plunging back into her pussy in the next moment, the real treat to him. She moaned lusciously, quivering where she was, her back rounded when she wanted to arch, yet her anatomy was such that she only enjoyed so much flexibility and range of potion in that area. What Theresa could do was grind back against him, however, saliva slopping out of her muzzle around the length of his cock, teeth carefully kept away from his shaft, even though there was nothing really that she could have done to hurt him. She'd sucked his cock far too many times for that to ever be an issue.

"Yes… Unff… My slutty dragoness…"

She was getting to him, though he plunged his tongue into her pussy and twirled it around, lapping up her essence, in such a way that Theresa didn't hear what he said next. The sensation was too intoxicating, her legs wet with her juices, too much pleasure coursing through her to be held. It was with a muffled cry around his cock, his dick acting as a better gag than they could fashion, that she climaxed, pussy rippling and pulsing, her body in that way designed perfectly for milking a male's shaft. It was rhythmic, each pulse coming with more power than the last, as if her body could not anticipate a time where she would not want to milk him of every drop of his seed.

Yet, even through orgasm, she needed it all so badly, moaning, grunting, nothing more than a mindless feral dragoness in heat, her body desperate for him. The scent of her filled the air, almost enough to overpower his musk, though the throbbing of his cock in her maw and throat ached for more, pre-cum spilling unendingly down her throat. It pooled hotly in her stomach even as climax ripped through her, her tail lashing back and forth to such an extent that Alister had to brace and pin it down, just to make sure that it would not catch him in the side of his muzzle inadvertently.

"Slutty dragonesses like you only need one…thing…unff…don't you, whore?"

Yes… Yes, oh, yes, she was his whore, his kinky whore, only Alister's whore. She quivered, though could not help but moan as Alister withdrew his cock from her muzzle, leaving her gaping, dripping with saliva and pre-cum, swirls of creamy fluid strung out between her teeth, showing where the thickness of it differed from her saliva. Yes, she wanted it, all his dirty words, his dominating language, though her mind swirled, as if she could not focus on any single thing.

What was she doing? Worshipping his nuts? Taking his cock? Oh, it didn't matter anymore, her need high, running rampant, her body aching for it as if her scales were going to crawl right off her body if she didn't get what she wanted. She was desperate for it, mewling, lapping and slavering over his cock as if there was nothing at all left for in the world, nothing that she could ever bear to pay more attention to than his hard, throbbing length.

"Now, now, my slut…"

That was the moment for Alister to take complete and utter control, grunting deep in the back of his throat, his flanks reverberating. A line of muscle showed down his side where his abdominal muscles contracted, though she would not be privy to that for much longer as he spun his slutty dragoness about, handling her as easily as he would a prey item. Yet Theresa was far more than that to him, so much more, her body primed and ready, her blistering scent scorching the air. There was a fire in her that could only be sealed away by the throbbing thrust of his cock, driving deep, stretching her open, spreading her wide, though there would be no need for any additional lubrication.

Theresa was always dripping for him, her chest pinned to the ground as he covered her body with his, the mindless dragoness keening out shrilly as the head of his cock brushed up against her vent.

"Yes… Master… Master! Fuck meeeeee!"

She screamed as he slammed in, having lined up, and penetrated her with half his cock in a single thrust, forcing her to accept his meat. The strain was immense as she howled, bucking and grinding, losing herself in the moment as she scared twilight birds from the trees, ones that were roosting for the night and those that were rousing for what was their most active time. But neither dragon cared one bit about those they disturbed, Alister thrusting, driving in deep, the strain of her pussy around him only inciting him to thrust harder.

He had to penetrate her, Theresa understood that, a helpless dragoness under him. That was entirely of her own doing, but there was nowhere else that the dragoness would rather have been, grunting and moaning, her tail winding around his leg, for she could not reach all the way back to his, where it thrashed, cracking into trees. An age-old oak creaked and crashed down into the undergrowth, but neither dragon paid it any mind, his rampant, overpowering thrusts stretching her out increasingly with every thrust.

More of his cock… Closer and closer, he bottomed out inside her, cramming the full length of his devout meat up to her innermost barrier. He could go deeper, especially with a dragoness as stretchy and as accommodating as she was, though Alister had no intention either of hurting her. Yet the slut liked it rough too, only an inch of his cock remaining outside her cunt, right up where his sheath-slit was strained taut.

He moaned, his rumbling cry echoing over her, neither dragon hiding their lust, their ardent passion for each other. It had to come out, all one way or another, her hind legs quivering even as she tried so very desperately to keep her hips raised for his lust and pleasure. There was no other moment for it, no other reason, squealing and gasping breathlessly, though Theresa could not draw enough breath into her lungs either, not for what she needed to do. All the dragoness was aware of was how fucking *good* it all felt, his driving thrusts grinding through her, feeling as her whole lower body was stretched out by him.

Maybe not quite that extreme…yet she would have done it all over again if that was what it meant for the lust of her master, the tryst of lovers. For dominance could be spent in true love too, the trust they had between them allowing them to go further, to trust each other more. They would never go further than one another's limits, even if the power dynamic of their relationship was set, moaning, grunting, thrusting and grinding as if there was no tomorrow. As if it was the last fuck they would ever get, their passion greater than they could ever have imagined.

He thrust as if his life depended on it, her head hazy, lost in orgasm after orgasm. Time no longer had any meaning for the lust-addled dragoness, whimpering, moaning, groaning, her nose tipping submissively to the ground. It didn't matter to Theresa whether she rose again with grass stains on her snout, only that she gave her master everything he wanted. Her body was merely a toy to him, yes, a hole for him to use, for it was not as if he had never taken her arse before either.

Whether her cunt or her tail hole… A hole was a hole to both of them, something for pleasure, something for lust, something for passion. That was all they needed as she groaned out his name, gutturally, deeply, so lowly that the syllables could barely be heard through it. The dragoness rolled her hips back, yet the pounding thrusts for the drake were merely to be borne, Alister taking her harder and faster, urgency in the heavy strokes of his cock.

He roared, tail lashing, striking down another tree in a splinter of branches and a crash of leaves, yet his orgasm was not to be stopped, not even as he forced the weight and muscle of his body down over her, heaving and panting, his sides reverberating with the force of every snatched breath. Alister blasted out his lust, bellowing it to the treetops and tips of the mountains watching on, yet each pulse of cum from his huge balls was sent directly into the womb of his dragoness. Bloating her up, overfilling her, her flanks swelling with every pump.

She moaned, laying her cheek down against the grass, though she didn't care, only for the sense of fullness, her belly swinging, as if she was several months pregnant already with a clutch of eggs. The weightiness of it was indulging, intoxicating, setting her to roll her hips back at him, claws digging into the dirt. In that moment it was more important than ever that she braced to take every pulse of his cock, his cum, his sweet dragoness twitching around him. She thought about herself that way, forgetting even her own name at the moment that it felt like it mattered the most, moaning and whimpering, grunting thickly, passion overcoming all else.

But she would still be there at the end of it all as he bloated out her stomach more and more, her belly swelling with his seed, fatter and rounder, inflated by his lust. Balls that big, after all, had quite a load for her, and her belly hung down, squashing against the ground, need pumping through, cum gurgling in her womb. She had to take it all, however, even as he rested there, his balls empty of his first load, though there would be even more to come, more passion, more thrusting. Alister was, after all, a very giving master…

Theresa shivered, the warmth of his body teasing into her, fuelling her passion. As much as she tried, however, she could not squeeze down on his cock anymore, her body brutally stretched, all as she wanted it to be.

"Master… Please… Take me…"

Alister rumbled a growl, his cock still hard inside her, keeping her open for him.

"You may worship me all night, slut…"

Theresa shivered, tongue dangling out of her mouth as she moaned. There was nowhere else she'd rather have been.

Only with her master.

Double Teamed by Gryphons

Minnie whimpered, the anthro dragoness splayed out on the beach with her breath trapped in her throat, as much as she wanted to ease the tension in her lungs. At the eve of the day, the last rays of crimson sunset splashed the ocean in their touch, her white scales offset by it, though her slender, elegant horns, which looked more like a red deer's antlers, enhanced her figure even more.

She knew what she was doing, even as the black shapes circled above, more than one of them. There was little light left in the close of the day and yet she knew exactly what she was doing, why she was allowing her bare scales to get grit and sand into the edges of them down on the beach.

"Yes... Please..."

She breathed, lips parted, pressing her her hind paws into the sand, digging into it as she arched her stomach and chest up in a tabletop position.

"Take me..."

She wanted them, so much. It was not right for a dragoness like her to strike out from the town where she lived (city life had never appealed) but she had done it anyway. It was her time, her weekend, her day out on the coast down Cornwall, though the smuggler's cove that she had climbed down into, precariously, was not one where she would be disturbed. Only the incoming tide could harry her and it was worth risking it for the gryphons circling overhead.

One black and one brown: their shapes became increasingly distinct as they descended, lazily spiralling as if they wanted her to see them in their glory first. Although Minnie could see somewhat in the night, twilight was a difficult time for her eyes, as was dawn, further ramping up the edge of danger in the situation, her heart pounding, cliffs towering darkly above. There was no way that she could get herself out of danger there in a hurry, but Minnie understood too that any danger in her head was of the manufactured kind, the kind that made her want to whimper and submit, just like that.

The good kind. The kind that came paw in paw with kink, her tail dragging in the sand under her, even as she lowered herself, arms aching, back to the sand. She cried out softly, her long, elegant jaws parting, though rolling her body onto all fours as the gryphons landed merely demonstrated her need, her intent framed as she pushed her quivering, lithe tail up over her back. The tip was shaped like a heart, if one looked at it closely enough, pointing to her head, her lips obediently parted even as her body ached with need.

Minnie didn't even know what the gryphons would like from her yet. And, still, she presented herself and her body to them in all ways as if she knew them intimately, as if they could not want anything other than her body. Yet those that frequented the Cornish coast knew well enough what those that ventured out alone, begging for attention, wanted.

Put simply, tourists were one thing when it came to Cornwall. Those seeking to satisfy lust of a more carnal, intimate variety would find themselves, down there, well taken care of.

Minnie held her breath as the gryphons settled into the sand, the brown beast adorned with glossy, rich feathers and a head that was like that of an eagle crossed with perhaps a larger breed of owl, tufts above his eyes, which were alight with need. His fur softened to a chocolate-like brown, though she wouldn't have liked to make that comparison out loud, not even as her pussy moistened with need, pearls of desire dripping down her soft folds.

The second gryphon was larger still, near the size of a horse with something thick already pushing from between his hind legs that made her heart leap. For where Minnie was an anthro dragoness, the gryphons were all feral and all male, studs in the best sense of the term. Some integrated with society, but who would really want to when that meant that they would have to live by anthro rules and no longer live the free, relaxed lives that they got down there on the coast?

No… The gryphons had it better. And Minnie's lust-addled body, trembling with heat, burning up from the inside out, needed something from them, a little something that meant that she might learn from their way of living. Just a little bit. Maybe.

"Brother, it seems that we have found a snack."

The black gryphon smirked – well, as well as any gryphon could smirk, having a beak instead of lips that were more flexible for such expressions. His head was smooth, a shocking yellow beak rising forth, though she whimpered at the sight of the hook-like tip. He could hurt her, if he wanted to, yet his eyes were kind, softening as he lowered his head to hers.

"What are you looking for, little female?"

Minnie shivered.

"I…" The words stuck in her throat. "I need… I need you…"

She blushed, her white scales showing the heat under them very obviously, warmth sweeping down from her cheeks across her neck in clinging, blotchy patches. But the gryphons had seen more than enough anthros like her sneaking down to the shore and even up and over the moors for their lusts, chuckling softly, shaking out his wing feathers as his leonine tail swept back and forth.

"Relax, breeder hen… We'll show you what you've been missing."

"And leave your belly nice and swollen."

Minnie made a sound that might have been a moan, but it was hard to tell with so much going on, the gryphons pairing up together, one on either side of her. Brother gryphons too! She could see the family resemblance in them, how they held themselves, the pride in their bodies, the set of their heads.

Yet none of that mattered as a beak pushed under her tail, which was still willingly raised, and the brown gryphon's needy shaft quested at her jaws. She parted them further, marvelling, if only for a moment, at the thick girth of him, though she was too far gone to know what she was doing, moaning aloud, her head spinning, lust coursing through with every beat of her heart.

What was to come would come and there was nothing more that Minnie felt that she could or would do about that. She had to be there, lust there, a beak under her tail, tongue flickering insistently into her pussy as it pushed deep.

"Mmmph… She's tight."

But she was not a virgin. That was the only thing that Minnie lamented, but she would not have enjoyed her visits and forays down to the south coast to see the gryphons so much if it was her first time every time. Wait, that didn't make sense, though it was hard for her to ever make any sense at all when there was a hot tongue curling into her pussy, her jaws parting wider and wider around a thick, smooth length of cock.

Oh, he was magnificent as the brown gryphon powered into her maw, trusting her to take him, confident that he would not be harmed by her teeth, as much of a risk as they were when it came to dragons. He thrust and ground, the tip of his cock a little tapered but more rounded, the type of dick that was a little more difficult, typically, for someone to take, but would still come right in the end. Minnie whimpered, lashing her tongue around it, though the long, flexible length could barely wrap entirely around the girthy meat of him, a stud gryphon drake who was more than worthy of the name.

And the tongue in her pussy, even dragging up and over her tail hole, was doing weird and wonderful things to her, pushing into her, dragging over her folds, pulling them apart as if he was only teasing her. Yet her fingers curled luxuriously into the sand as that special kind of pleasure washed over her, the kind that made her feel giddy in the pit of her stomach, light-headed, as if she was going to be caught up in the rising tide.

The water was still far enough away not to be a risk as true night fell, the gryphons shrouded in darkness while her sharp eyes picked out all the light they could, defining them in detail, even down to the edges of their feathers. Minnie whimpered, head spinning, a gryphon cock driving into the back of her throat and deeper as she gulped and swallowed around it, suppressing her gag reflex the best she could. It still made her eyes water, yet it was a delicious feeling to her, something drawing tighter and tighter inside her, breath catching, need rising.

"Mmm, she's going to be a good fuck, brother."

Minnie moaned. Oh, please, oh, please… More, deeper, more… One gryphon cock pounded her throat, driving into the fleshiness of it with a huge, thick bulge. The dragoness could only shudder beneath them, her entire attention focused on how they filled her, stroke after stroke of the brown gryphon's cock powering into her maw, her throat. She didn't know their names and yet she didn't have to know them, grunting in the back of her throat, eyes closing.

No longer did she think about where she was, the beach, the feel of the gritty sand under her paws. All she could do was grind back on that tongue as it lapped and slurped, pushing into her, spreading her open, as if she even needed to be prepared. No, she was already ready, had been ready from the moment that she cast her clothes aside in the shadows of the cliff, baring it all.

Her pussy dripped, yet any moisture that spilt was lapped up by the gryphon. She could not help but notice how he pulled at her folds, tugging over her clit, as he lapped and she moaned.

"Oohhhhh… Mmmmph…"

No, she couldn't say anything and neither did they care about her saying anything at all, as long as she was willing, grinding onto them, her throat bulging out with stroke after stroke of gryphon meat. The brown gryphon leaned over her head, pushing her down, forcing her to submit even while her submission had already, so very readily, been given. Yet she was right where she wanted to be even as something tightened in the pit of her belly, straining and trembling until it could not resist breaking.

Her cries went unnoticed as she took down every bit of his cock, letting his crotch grind into her nose, pussy twitching around the other gryphon's tongue. The black gryphon moaned and shuddered, pressing against her even more urgently, need coursing through. She could only imagine how hard and throbbing his cock was already, wanting her, her folds dripping as he drew back, inhaling deeply through the nares on his beak.

"Mmm… As if you weren't ready, dragoness."

Yes, yes, that was right, Minnie was ready, so very much so, moaning, whimpering, though her cries were muffled as her head swam with the afterglow of pounding orgasm. Dimly, she was aware of him pushing over her back, his weight on her, though he must have taken more weight back on his hind legs too, or else he would have pleasurably crushed her into the ground. Not that she felt like she would have minded much, the power of a male like him, dominant and overpowering, his cock pressing into her pussy.

He didn't need to thrust or to jab as he drove home, his cock sliding easily into her, stretching her tight folds around him. Minnie moaned, though her head swirled, her pussy aching, orgasm tearing through her. It was not a gentle, warming kind of orgasm either, but the kind that snatched her up and, if she had been airborne like the gryphons had been not so long ago, would have tossed her down to the jaws of the ocean below. It claimed her, her body twisting, wanting to contort, anything to bear through the power of the pulsating twitches of her pussy, how her passage slopped and dripped around his pounding length.

The gryphons did not care. Her orgasm was none of their concern, but merely a side effect of what they took from her, slamming in, grind after grind, double-teaming her from both ends. The brown gryphon huffed and puffed through his nares as he slammed into her throat, forcing her to accept it, though she was right where she wanted to be, her vision blocked out by the undercarriage of the gryphon, his soft, brown fur and strong hindquarters more than enough to make her swoon.

Yet the black gryphon, his brother, slammed into her confidently, dominance oozing from him. When it came to gryphons, they never had to pretend to be something that they were not, not even the once, her passage opening up around him, welcoming his length in, though he was thicker at the base than his brother. A bulge that had to pound into her as he ground it right up against her pussy lips, stretching them open, getting her to accept him, even though the slurping wetness of her folds begged his attention anyway.

Minnie was there for a reason, her pussy closing around him, rippling, pulling, wanting more to milk him of his seed, no longer at all feeling in her right mind as she enjoyed the moment. It was what she was there for, after all, whimpering and groaning, her cries muffled in the softness of the night and their harsh taking of her. Harder, she wanted to tell them, please, take me harder. She was not there for the lightness and the gentleness that they could have given her, but a pounding, snarling claiming that would leave her with a clutch of eggs in her womb at the end of it all.

She needed it, craved it, was desperate for it. Her co-workers, on her return, might whisper about what she'd done, whether there was a husband or not, but she didn't care. She was not a dragoness that cared one bit about the opinions of sheep when she had the teeth to chase them away – that was if she even heard them. She was far more interested in seeing what could come from the fruits of her labour, how far she could take her life in the search and pursuit of such passion.

The drive of their cocks, the one in her throat inching a touch deeper while the bulge popped in and out of her pussy, so thick and so heady… Her mind drifted, not able to follow one line of thought. What more could a dragoness want as she moaned around them, delivered through orgasm after orgasm, panting, heaving, her tail pushed up still as far over her back as she could manage.

"Yes, dragoness… You belong to us now."

She could not tell which of them climaxed first, for all Minnie knew was that she was awash in a sea of pleasure, swamping her, pouring over her, howling, crying out, wanting it all the more, always more. She gulped, before the cum spurted out the corners of her lips, but her pussy could only take every drop of creamy seed that she was given, driving deep, seeding her full.

To be impregnated, to be taken… Her head swam with pleasure, her body aching, tingling, feeling as if she had swum for miles upon miles. There was no going back, not even if she tried to take a "morning after" pill, for they did not work on the power of a feral gryphon, their seed pumping too deep and too quickly to be stopped.

But Minnie had never wanted a choice in the matter, giving over her submission to them so much more than willingly, grunting, groaning, lost in the moment.

It was the best place to be, forgetting her life, where she'd been, everything that she had been. She would be so much more as their hot seed poured into her, pooling in the pit of her stomach as she swallowed it all down, throat working furiously to take it all where it needed to be. The bulge tugged lightly at her folds as if the gryphon had been locked into her, though he could still pull out at any time. The difference there was that she didn't want him to leave her empty, not at all, crying out softly, warmth flooding her body, right down to the tips of her fingers and toes.

When she came back around, she had locked her limbs, braced on the sand, which was more than a little torn up around her body. The black gryphon slopped his still hard dick free of her pussy, though they were not done with her yet.

For she was there to serve their needs, to do everything for them that they asked for her, to be bred repeatedly until the gryphons too were certain that their bloodlines had, once again, been passed on into another needy dragoness. The brown gryphon was more forceful, nipping at her backside, forcing her tail back up and out of the way where it had drooped, though her lust was still there, swelling in the back of her mind.

If they were not done with her, the dragoness could not be done with them.

"My brother may have had your pussy once, dragoness," he hissed, bearing her down into the sand as his cock jabbed, questing for her pussy. "But you haven't been bred by me yet either…"

Minnie moaned, relaxing, tail trying to twitch up out of the way, all to make her body more accessible to him. Yes, yes, always yes, always when it came to the gryphons. He purred, rumbling above her, brown feathers quivering as his flanks shuddered.

"There's a good dragoness…"

Always, for them, only for them.

As his cock probed at her bare, drooling cunt, leaking the remnants of his brother's orgasm, Minnie knew that there was no way she was going to leave her time there without a womb fool of seed, ready and impregnated, as fertile as she was. She couldn't wait to see how her stomach would swell in the coming months, bearing the fruit of new life.

He bore her into the ground, penetrating her deeply. Minnie's cries echoed off the cliffs, all while his brother looked on.

And she wouldn't have wanted it any other way.

Knots

The German Shepherd smirked as he loomed over Lacey's body, the mare stretched out and quivering before him in shibari bondage. There was nothing more beautiful to Stanley than his partner all stretched out on the bed before him, even if their play in domination and submission allowed him to be somewhat of a harsher partner than he was normally.

Lacey's chest heaved, the strikingly marked appaloosa huffing and panting through flared, pink nostrils. Her white coat hid pink skin and her tail was bound and wrapped up in a tail bandage so he could easily access the plush, pink folds of her pussy and her doughnut-like tail hole. The mare's black spots marked a white hide and her arms had been pulled up over her head, tied off to the headboard of the bed. With her hooves stretched out with a spreader bar between the knees, she was effectively helpless yet in a position where he could turn her to the side or lift her legs up some to get at her anal pucker a little more easily, if he wanted to.

"My dear…"

He growled playfully, though the mare's ears only twitched, trying to catch where he was in the room. He would have loved to look into her blue eyes, but a blindfold was too tempting, just to add that extra note of sensory deprivation for her. Depriving her of one sense heightened the others and Stanley licked his lips in a lewd, wet swipe of his tongue as his hackles prickled and his tail tried to wag behind him. Sometimes that was one reason he blindfolded her: he was too telling with his tail, showing how much he was enjoying it all when a more dominant persona suited the moment more.

Still, he was used to slipping into different roles as they explored the lure of BDSM, always with a safe word ready in case it was ever needed. It was better to have it and never need to use it rather than to struggle to know how to stop a scene.

"Mmmm... Please... You've teased me for so long..."

She moaned, trying to arch up, though Lacey could not hold the arch in her lower back for too long, quivering in place. The strain on her body was delicious and a part of Stanley wished too he could feel exactly what she was experiencing, even if being in the bottom role wasn't quite what he wanted either. There was just so much more to the moment than a limited point of view and he hungered to experience every last little scrap of feeling in the world he could glean for himself.

"Ah-ah," he murmured, his tone rough and low, as if a growl was threatening even then. "I don't need you to do anything else, my filly. Just you lay there, let me take you."

The rope bondage crisscrossed her body, framing her breasts nicely with the pink nipples standing out, perky in the cool air of the bedroom. The rest of the room was cast into a soft darkness with only the bedside lamp illuminating the room, the safety scissors set there too. It was a small precaution but one he liked to have there for them both, in case he needed to snip through the ropes in a hurry.

She twisted in her bondage, the ropes coming under her buttocks to show off her rump, though she looked like she wanted to lift her legs for him. Stanley didn't need that, however, not yet, the canine bare but for his fur as his cock swelled.

"So many knots..." He murmured, tracing the path of the rope bondage all over her body. "So many... And I have one more for you here, if you will be a good filly for me."

"Mmm, yes, Master," she nickered readily, trying to squirm even as she tugged on her wrist restraints.

"Yes, I'll do anything for you, I'll be good! I promise I'll be good."

She licked her lips, putting emphasis on "good," though Stanley knew she liked to rile him up too, pushing the boundaries. It was all part of their play as Lacey found comfort in knowing he would readily reinforce the boundaries if she ever came up against them, secure in mental bonds as well as physical ones.

"Mm, well, you won't get it inside you if you're not good, so I hope you mean that, filly."

She quivered and moaned as he got on with the show, playing with her pussy as he slid his fingers up along the soft folds of her sex. Mares had a different shaped sex than many other anthros and the teardrop shape had always fascinated Stanley. But the dog maintained his composure as he smirked, rubbing her pussy and toying with the fat bud of her clit as it easily showed her arousal.

Her moans were music to his ears, though Stanley felt he didn't have to do all that much when it came to her. The lightest of touches had her pussy dampening in a sheen of arousal, though he had teased her beforehand. It was his fingers parting the folds of her pussy to show it off to her that had the mare squirming and nickering, begging without words for him to push inside her.

Yet Stanley held back, his tongue lolling briefly from his mouth in a pant. The German Shepherd's tail lifted and he tensed his glutes as his cock throbbed, a drop of pre-cum beading at the tip. He was not overly productive as a typical rule, but Stanley hadn't got off that week while work took over, which left him more pent up than usual.

"My pretty filly… Whinny for me, maybe then I'll give you what you need."

What she craved was the knot and only the knot – and not the ones crisscrossing her body in shibari bondage. The mare nickered and bobbed her head, her nostrils flaring as she let loose a high-pitched whinny.

"Please, Master, take me," she begged, assuming correctly she was allowed. "I need you, I need your big cock so badly! I need you inside me… Please, don't just tease me, use me. I'm yours to be used, however you please, oh, please…"

She gulped hard, ears twitching, before she lost herself entirely. The canine smirked, lips twitching. Oh, how he enjoyed her moods. There was something sweeter about her submission than ever before that night, as if they were both coming home to something they had needed and yet not found the time to experience.

Perhaps the land of domination and submission offered them more relief in which to express themselves than they could have otherwise realised.

Only time would tell as he dipped his fingers into her sex, pressing two digits together as he curled them up lightly. Dragging his short claws through her sex, he rubbed the smooth, filed tips against her G-spot, taking only a few moments to find that part of her pussy where the texture shifted. It was hard to describe, though, to him, it felt as if there was simply a touch more friction in that area, which always helped Stanley nail the spot that drove her wild.

"Mmph – oh!"

The mare under him squealed and tried to twist, though her legs were still mostly pushed out before her with her knees slightly bent. The spreader bar between her knees kept her legs apart, though it was a time where Lacey may well have tried to close them, if only to tease herself by squeezing her thighs together around the plush heat of her pussy.

Her reactions were what he craved, however, from the tiny twitches in her body and the tensing of her muscles. She tried so hard to please him, to be the submissive he wanted – even if there was a prize in store for her.

So, Stanley played her body, keeping her on the edge once the heat within her had built. It didn't take long, his two fingers slick with her juices, his thumb brushing her clit – though only lightly. If he went too hard, she'd get off straight away and then it wouldn't have been quite as fun for both of them.

His cock throbbed wantonly and Stanley reminded himself to hold back a little more, even as he thumbed the head of his cock. Smearing the pre-cum around the tip, he laughed lightly. There'd be no issue at all in pushing into his mare and he knelt on the bed, poised over her while his paw stayed back down over her crotch, working his fingers shallowly inside her.

"Do you think you've earned this first knot, my dear?" He growled, suddenly pressing in hard to elicit a yelp from her. "There's many more rounds in store for you, tied to me, unable to do anything but twist and squirm, my pony to do with as I please."

"Yes – please!" She cried out, bucking her hips up against his paw, doing her best to get even a jot more stimulation. "Please… Fuck me, Master! Knot me!"

It was all she could force out and Stanley pushed over her, even if it was his own will he was obeying. She'd have more than one knotting that night, over and over again, until her pussy was stretched lewdly, gaping in the absence of him with a dripping cream-pie. But that was for her to discover as minutes passed into hours, his cock spearing into her as he pinned her down to the bed in a mating press. Her legs were forced out straight, still parted, as he drove into her, the fat length of his cock filling her as his mare had wanted all along.

She may have cried out, but he pushed his ears back solely to protect them, for anthro ears, as a general rule, were quite sensitive. The mare under him shuddered as ripples of lust rolled through her, her pussy gripping and pulling around his cock, though Stanley knew with due certainty she was not in control of her own body.

She didn't need to be. Not as he pounded into her with smooth, commanding strokes, falling into a rhythm that suited him, though he put an extra jab of savagery into his thrusts, even though it wouldn't land with her at all in the heat of passion. She would beg for more, if she wanted rougher play from him and he was more often than not too gentle for her.

That was where his control came into play, however, making her beg for the crude, overpowering strokes that had her melting into a puddle of lust. He could hold her on the edge for hours if the notion took his fancy – or push her through orgasm after orgasm, all to see her come undone before him.

Yet the moment was about Stanley too as he sealed the deal for his first orgasm of the night, shoving his half-inflated knot into the swollen heat of her sex. Once inside, it pumped up fully, pushing against the bounds of her pussy, and Lacey squealed all over again, bucking and twitching under him, though she was barely able to move an inch or so under his body.

He ground into her with short, sharp thrusts, keeping his cock deep while the knot stopped him from pulling out. Lacey's cunny clenched on it, her slickness softening the edge of friction, as she cast herself into another orgasm. A whinny tore itself from her, so high-pitched it cut through the air, and he panted heavily, muttering a curse as he slammed deep and lost himself inside her.

There was nothing to hold him back, not in knotting her, bowing his head to her neck to nip at her throat while he spent his seed inside her. His cream left him in long, hot spurts of cum, filling her pussy, though not a single drop leaked out from the tight seal his knot made where their bodies joined.

In knotting lust, there was much pleasure to be had, though he stayed there, savouring every single moment. From the pull of her pussy around his knot, massaging it purely from the draw of orgasm, to the tremor of her breasts against his chest, all he longed to do was to soak it all in.

Every moment held its own importance, power surging through him as he cupped her cheek softly, letting her lean into his touch to make it firmer.

Knotted inside her, he would not deflate for some time. With many of their favourite toys within reach, in the bedside drawers, they had plenty to stay occupied with.

"My pretty mare…"

Yes, he thought hazily. *There's nowhere else I'd rather be than knotted with you.*

BDSM demanded trust. But, for them, it brought a sweeter sense of closeness and intimacy that they otherwise could not have enjoyed.

Thank you for reading and I hope that everything was very much enjoyed!

Ready for more? Check out my author website for more furry fiction and where you can purchase my books!

https://linktr.ee/amethystmare

Cover art illustrated by verysweetpotato; they are contactable via Twitter for work enquiries.

twitter.com/AlexandrCorvin